VERA VIOLET

VERA VIOLET

A Novel

MELISSA ANNE PETERSON

COUNTERPOINT
Berkeley, California

Vera Violet

Library of Congress Cataloging-in-Publication Data
Names: Peterson, Melissa Anne, 1981– author.
Title: Vera Violet : a novel / Melissa Anne Peterson.
Description: First paperback edition. | Berkeley, California : Counterpoint, 2020.
Identifiers: LCCN 2019014913 | ISBN 9781640092327
Classification: LCC PS3616.E84348 V47 2020 | DDC 813/.6—dc23
LC record available at https://lccn.loc.gov/2019014913

Cover design by Nicole Caputo
Book design by Jordan Koluch

COUNTERPOINT
2560 Ninth Street, Suite 318
Berkeley, CA 94710
www.counterpointpress.com

Printed in the United States of America
Distributed by Publishers Group West

10 9 8 7 6 5 4 3 2 1

To my parents,
Melody and Scott,
who always helped me

VERA VIOLET

HELL OUT OF DODGE

The Montana sky opened up and gave me snow. Snow to numb my wounds. Snow to cover my footprints. Snow to cushion the echo of the rifle as I fired it repeatedly.

Eventually, my target became shredded and my pocket empty of bullets. I gathered my debris and sat on my tailgate. I watched the patient conifers gather white snowflakes. I was alone except for lodgepole pine and grand fir. I knew that if I lay down underneath the branches, the green needles would hide my body. If I curled up there, I would soon freeze. Scavengers would eat my flesh. But the trees would remain, untouched. Because my survival meant nothing. I would always be a wild thing crouching. Jubilant only for brief moments during times of plenty. Comfort was ephemeral. Passion short-lived.

On the bench seat of my rusty white Ford was a .40-caliber handgun and a letter with ancient creases. I propped the rifle against the dashboard and climbed in next to the handgun and piece of paper. I tapped the snow from my boots and slammed the door. I had to crank the engine twice before it rumbled to life. At first the heater blew out cold air but soon the snow from my wool gloves melted onto the paper. I reread the words I had already memorized. The frantic pencil lines were faded and smudged. But they stood out plainly in the reflected light from winter snow:

Vera Violet (my fighter),

I'm staying here for a while, and I'm giving you this handgun (with 16 in the magazine). I have my sharpened, stainless steel blades, a compound hunting bow, graphite arrows, and a leather quiver. I have a cellar filled with these things (in a cabin on Granny's property). I'll save my pencils and notebooks. I'll repeat my words and weigh them. I'll lace my boots and visit the gravel pit to sight the rifles in and oil the barrels.

I'm staying here to hunt. I'll fish and gather berries and roots. There will be no disconnection between my body and the bodies of others. Between my food and the deer running. Between my pen and my ancestors or my boots and the dirt.

I'll fix my old truck and hope for the best. But I'll prepare for the worst (when the credit runs out and someone has to start making payments). I know the time will come (it always does). I know it when the ocean tides ebb, and Oakland Bay looks weary. That's when I see how the rats and coyotes and raccoons prepare themselves. They gather to feast. They get ready for the great selling-out (the going back on agreements . . . when everybody's soft belly shows).

I think the worst will come when the silver jets take off for the last time. That's when the false fronts crumble and the past will reappear. I imagine those dead men and women rising, Hypochaeris and Scotch broom blossoming, the sun burning and maddening. That's when the plastic melts and bubbles, cities burn to the ground, and the soft-handed men look back to see what is left.

Only then, when their suits are torn to rags (when dirty fingernails dig in barren soil blindly). Only then, will they see us. Entire families. Like cockroaches. Like we always were. Each man, woman, and child with two feet planted in the too-real soil. Guarding our little piece. Fingers on our triggers. Smiling.

I know it's hard. I know you're sad. But I also know these things will happen. Go find Mother. I'll be there soon. Just keep your weapon near you (with 16 in the magazine).

—Dad

I finished reading and refolded the paper. I put it back into the glove box with the unloaded handgun and full magazine.

One thousand miles away, the O'Neel family swampland gathered water. Fifth-wheel trailers slid down hillsides. Cabins sunk deeper into the soft, wet soil. My father struggled up a brambly hillside in the rain. He was hurried and anxious—desperately following the sloppy trail of a buck in a death-run who stumbled while bleeding. It was growing dark in Western Washington. Mosquitoes whined in the wet shadows that spread. A mountain lion smelled the fresh blood and screamed.

I got out of the truck and crouched on the frozen ground in Montana. I took out my buck knife and slashed lines into the cold earth at my feet. The lines turned into letters, and when I finally turned my back to leave, a message was temporarily carved into the icy soil: *It has been very hard to love you.*

Within minutes the sound of my engine died away. The words carved into the bitter ground were seen only by a hesitant bobcat who sniffed warily. Snow soon covered my tire tracks, and the sentence was lost forever.

PART 1

1

FIGHTERS

A long time ago, a scowling face with shaggy dark hair stared up at me during recess. The new boy wanted me to come down from the big wooden tower. He yelled with scrubbed hands cupped around a red mouth. The wind took away his words.

Tanya, Tammy, and Sherrie stood around the thick pine logs with crossed arms. They would not let the new boy through. Because *I* was the leader. And *I* said who could climb the ladder to the top.

I beat the boy after school. I did not say a word before or after. I beat him because he stood against the brick wall alone like he was a fighter. So I came up to him fast with a sucker punch. He doubled over, and I pushed him down. I gave him a swift kick for good measure.

As he lay in the mud gasping, I retreated and threw handfuls of pea gravel from the wooden tower where Tanya, Tammy, and Sherrie waited. It rained down on his curled form as he struggled for air. The fistfuls of small rocks were meant to tell him: *I* am a fighter. *I* was born for this.

My body was tall and gangly. I was boyish and ugly with holey jeans and dirty clothing. I had devil-colored yellow hair that hung down in long greasy strands. Insatiable blue eyes. A face that glared.

My teacher sent a note home to Mother. It told her I was "negatively influencing the other female students." And I "incited them to violent acts."

Mother told me I had to stop and slapped me hard. She gave me extra chores. My brother, Colin, laughed. My sister, Mima, scoffed. My cheek burned and felt puffy where Mother's hand slapped my face. But my wooden tower was the best place. I knew I would go back there. Day after day.

Before I got on the school bus the next morning, Mother sighed and told me I did not fit my name: Vera Violet. "I named you after my mother and she was a gentle lady." She told me *Vera* was my grandmother's first name. And violet was the flower she loved best. A flower that grew in the prairies south of town. On mysterious humps of earth named mima mounds. Mother told me I didn't act like her mother or those little purple blooms. She knew deep inside that I could not stop fighting. That I was born for it.

When I got to school, the Fighter Boy got his revenge. He caught me at first recess. Real quick. He grabbed my arm and held it. It was picture day. They handed out little black combs for us to straighten our hair with. He had his in his front pocket. He took it out and swiped at my arm. He did it hard because I was squirming to get away. He used it like a knife. He got me right below the elbow where my skin was pulled taut.

He didn't think the black plastic would cut me. His eyes

popped open wide in surprise when it did. He watched the blood drip to my wrist. He dropped my arm like it was hot metal, stared ferociously into my eyes, and grinned. The next instant, he turned tail and ran. I held my fingers over the wound and stared after him. A calculating calm settled in my young mind.

That night, I dreamed of mima mounds covered in early blue violets. Undulating hills stretched on for miles. There was a zigzag fence. My black-and-white retriever ran beside me.

The Fighter Boy waited on a mound with his arms crossed—frowning. Fescue brushed his pant legs. Violets blinked their purple faces among the green bunchgrass. Flowers covered the hills as far as we could see.

Together, we walked through wet areas between mounds. We traveled deep. The standing water was warm and dark—it covered our knees. We slipped down farther, into a low spot between two bulges of earth. A space filled with calm and awe and secrets. A place of otherworldly hope and violence. Into the soil. The water heaved silently. It was over our heads. We were inside my female body. A womb. And it was filled with dark water.

I woke from the dream in a strange mood that lingered. The night had offered a sensation that changed me. In the morning, I went to my wooden tower first thing like always. I looked out at the playground from my cold, windy, queenly position. I knew I felt different. I knew, as the rain came down, I loved the Fighter Boy.

Small children are capable of great love. Love that overwhelms. Love that changes small worlds completely. Dangerous feelings that blot out everything.

That day, a rumor rippled up and down the hallways of the grade school: The Fighter Boy was kicked out of school forever.

The principal insisted on it. He saw how the Fighter Boy smashed the face of the older fifth grader (the would-be bully—the thief who robbed the Fighter Boy of his baseball cap).

The rain still poured after school let out. Kids shivered inside their raincoats in the bus lines. I saw Tanya, Tammy, and Sherrie standing with their hands on their hips in front of the wooden tower. They waited.

But I snuck out a hole in the back fence. I slid down the mud bank to the bottom where raging wastewater bubbled. I waited for my bus alone in the wet weeds. I threw rocks the size of pigeons into the muddy torrent of water. I counted the minutes out loud as I sat. My bus would take a long time yet.

Tanya, Tammy, and Sherrie finally came to find me. They had to sneak down one by one. We were all dirty and wet and pressed close together. They sat next to the water with me. We threw rocks the size of starlings. And sticks as thick as pencils. I told them about mima mounds and purple flowers. Tammy smoked a cigarette. They left one at a time to catch their buses. Mine was the last—rural routes always took the longest.

The wind picked up. My feet were numb inside my muck-caked rubber boots. My body grew stiff beside the stream of grimy runoff. I stayed there as the gusts blew my hair, the wind whipped the bare skin peeking through the holes in my jeans, and my ears grew red and ached. I listened to the breeze rustling the red alder leaves. I waited for the wind to carry the sound of the yellow school bus and the smell of diesel exhaust.

I waited for the wind to return to me the words it had stolen. When the Fighter Boy yelled up at me—with scrubbed hands cupped around a red mouth.

2

HILLBILLY MUSIC

My father was so good-looking he induced certain sounds in a viewer. His sideburns boasted reverb. His crooked smile was outlaw country music. The calluses on his palms made them rough-hewn lumber that boomed and thudded. His arms were heavy and powerful like Les Paul guitars.

I called him Dad, and he worked swing shift, so I didn't see him during the week. But on the weekends he told me stories in the driveway. I handed him tools while he hunched shirtless over his pickup that broke down a lot. He propped the hood open with a wooden stick, and I helped. It always took a long time.

After the note came home from my teacher, he told me different things than usual. He told me about the prisoners with shaved heads who weren't allowed to speak. In the hills among the big trees. The sawmills and logging camps. Douglas fir one thousand years old. I listened carefully to every word. I pictured shoulders hunched over loud machines. Blood boiling inside silent bodies. Anger. Frustration. Thick, dark forests. Before all the trees were cut down. Way back. That first white baby born in Washington Territory—a crying infant with no home. Dad talked about steep hillsides. Old growth. Men in shackles and chains. The blades screeching and moaning. Mountain devils waiting. Lumber barons with evil hearts, heavy pockets, and mouths salivating as they watched the prisoners die on cold windy floors. Their chains caught in the machinery. Their shaved heads a bloody symbol. Their scalps shorn with dull straight razors to stop the spread of lice, demoralize their hearts, and help them forget they were human.

He told me the men worked in leg-irons, and if their fingers caught in the blades, they were sometimes cut off with common carpenter saws. Dad shook his head and let me know "they didn't have doctors. Didn't have real prisons. They had those work camps at first. Couple rich fuckers wanted to get richer." He stared at me. A shotgun warning surged from his black Irish blue eyes before he said, "That's what greed does."

In my mind, the unspoken words huddled underneath the prisoners' thirsty tongues. Frustration erupted in their tired bodies. It coiled and raced and circled in fierce, red blood. Their words did not come out through crooked, set teeth. Clenched jaws halted. The men were voiceless. And their tongues stumbled clumsily even when free.

"And what about later?" I asked him.

He was quiet before he spoke. "Later, they buried the men where they died. In shallow, unmarked graves. Broken chains, falling logs, and violence killed them."

I imagined their blood mixing with the sawdust. I imagined

them falling asleep to the phantom nighttime hooting and chattering of northern spotted owl. The trees looming far above. The rain pouring down.

When Mother came home and found me in the driveway with big, wild thoughts in my head, she scolded him. Dad told me these things because he saw something in my eyes. A hunger that would remain. A hardness that must have meaning. He saw how I strutted when I walked.

My life would be difficult. I was a fighter. And I was born for it.

He oiled his boots at the foot of my bed as he talked before bedtime. He caught my eye before speaking. Sometimes, when I stared straight into his eyes in the dark I heard a fiddler playing notes in the devil's key. Sometimes, when I looked at how his black hair swept across his forehead, I heard wicked harmonicas telling secrets.

He told me that Wesley Everest was thrown off the bridge on Mellon Avenue three times before his neck finally snapped. And that young boys were taken out of town regularly and beaten one by one by men in city shoes. He told me that even as the workers' faces were filled with purple bruises, the desperate boys asked what right the lumber barons had to the land in the first place. They asked how they could steal and exploit so decadently. Wesley Everest hung from the bridge all night. His teeth broken and bloody—caved in with the butt of a rifle. The men castrated him and shot his body repeatedly. Dad told me that neither coroner in town would take the dead man in the morning. And no one was prosecuted for the murder. His jailed friends were forced at gunpoint to dig the hole where he was buried.

He told me that in New England hundreds of years ago Irish, Scottish, and poor English servants conspired together with African-born slaves to escape to freedom. He described the rebellions. And how afterward the masters forbid them to interact. And they were not allowed to marry one another. He said runaway slaves with light skin used to shave their heads to blend in. He explained to me that *white trash* was a name created for those who lived in mixed neighborhoods. It was a name for the poverty that remained in spite of skin color. He told me how rednecks were workers of all skin colors who protested unfair treatment. "Those words shouldn't hurt you." He patted my feet and turned my light down low. He set his boots against the doorframe.

Mom lingered in the hallway and listened. He walked toward her, and I could hear her reprimanding and him sighing. Her words, "Giving her confused nightmares," floated across my sleepy eyelids. I saw them spelled out. Colin snored lightly. My parents kissed in the dark.

Dad told me those things back when his truck still ran. When he was twenty-seven and good-looking. When he whistled and music played out of his radio in the driveway. When the future was bright and existed. Before we moved to Cota Street, I could fall asleep in the trailer in a clear-cut surrounded by other O'Neels. On those nights, I thought the wind chime was the rattling of the prisoners' chains. And my dreams were of business owners who slept lightly— their billy clubs waiting.

But in my dreams, the men with shaved heads had brilliant eyes. Even though they were ensnared. Even though they were never allowed to speak.

3

AS I GOT OLDER

We moved to Cota Street when I was nine. Cota kids were born of immigrants and nomads and peasants. There was never royal blood. The families were not written about in important books with hard covers. The struggles reached their steadfast fingers through each generation with precision. Every family was touched.

Sometimes, I thought my own immigrant nomad ancestors weren't really troubled. I imagined them relaxed and flexible—solving problems tenaciously. Good and faithful friends. Fighting and asking questions and making love long into the night. Sometimes, I thought of my great-great-uncles shouting curse words to the wet night sky and laughing. They must have known before me that nothing lasts forever. Not even the new buildings, massive trees, or frequent beatings. I imagined them searching for the wild lands and the wild things. I knew they understood, even as their deaths loomed closer, that someday they would rise again.

As I got older, the steelhead runs were not what they used to be. The big fish were near extinction. Natural resources dwindled down to the barest of bones. The forests that had once seemed to never end were shorn and overwhelmed. Corporations declared bankruptcy. Sold off their excess land. They finished with their liquidations and the mountainsides were left naked. Mini malls and developments popped up out of nowhere. The purple flowers were crowded out by introduced weeds. The butterflies flew away and did not come back.

I watched carefully as timberland became ritzy bedroom communities. The Esworthys, who bought our property after the bank foreclosed on my father, didn't know anything different. They paid me and Colin to tend the stretch of fertilized turf they installed in front of their house. I watched Mr. Esworthy fight private battles with nature using herbicides and clippers. The stream started to look strange.

Distant grocery stores with organic produce from other countries took the place of Mother's backyard garden. Her vegetables went to seed.

The Esworthys stayed on the highway that drove through town. They said they had no reason to visit the city of David. They swam in Wynoochee Lake, took pictures of moss-covered big-leaf maples, fished in the Hamma Hamma River, and gambled on the Squaxin Island reservation. Their wilderness was recreation. It was small and consumable. They conquered it with backpacks and hiking shoes. They had never seen an old-growth forest. Or been stalked by a wild thing.

The Esworthys smiled at my father's ragged shirt and work boots as if they were a funny costume he put on for them. His clothes were out-of-date. From an era long ago. He had worked hard for no reason. The state now had a capitol building and a college, and the timber money had been invested in enterprises we could never touch. My father, and other men like him, were no longer needed. They had little to show for the generations of missing body parts and hard labor.

The Esworthys owned our land now. They would not sell it back to us. A five-bedroom house was erected for the childless couple. It was their second home. They went to the salmon ceremony in August with cameras. Mrs. Esworthy chatted excitedly with Colin and me about the plans to pave the roads to several wilderness areas. She would soon be able to drive her commuter car all the way to the tops of mountains.

Colin and I looked at each other in alarm. I pushed my dirt-rimmed fingernails down into the soil and didn't answer. I knew the men who once owned the lumber companies had put on their expensive suits. And flown away in silver jets. The rain came in autumn like always.

The forests remained clear-cut. Bald hills turned to soupy messes that slid. The silt flowed into the rivers. Entire families of salmon died. Tributaries lost the ability to sustain life. Tourists held their noses against the smell of rotting fish carcasses. Grocery stores in small towns put up signs that read NO MORE CREDIT. Fishing rights that reservations had fought so hard for were almost useless. Their guns stayed in their holsters. It was hard to make a living from fishing anymore.

Downtown, the tidewater mill wasn't as busy as it used to

be. The mill workers stood around and shook their heads at the loss. Heavy fog hid the town. The angry prisoners deep inside had been forced into silence for more than a century. The Wobblies had been killed and imprisoned eighty years ago.

My father told my mother that he would try to "work harder," that it was just a "bad time." My mother planted a garden on Cota Street. My father tried to believe his boss paid him what he was worth. He was anxious. He wore his work boots through to the floor.

My brother and I stood beside him as he picketed in the parking lot of the mill where he had worked for fifteen years. We were out of school for the summer. I fished for sea-run cutthroat trout in Goldsborough Creek with a homemade fishing pole. My father's workmates did not grow angry and throw fists in the air. They held their signs in a deep, reserved silence. The price of lumber declined. Manufacturing moved overseas. Somewhere inside of them the workers wanted to believe the owners had hearts— that fairness would overcome. But the men with the money were long gone. Large tracts of land lay abandoned and muddy. The picket lines were futile. The damage was done. Greed won out. And the land could no longer support us.

Students from the state college poured salt in open wounds. They spit on our father's work trucks and protested a century too late. They didn't see the difference between loggers and the multi-million-dollar corporations. Thousands of men and women were out of work. The students didn't understand. They didn't know the children who waited in cabins without electricity and trailers without toilets. They didn't see the rotten vegetables of food bank food on scarred wooden tables or the long drives into town in rusty, rickety vehicles. They fought to protect the northern spotted owl, and old-growth timber that was mostly, already gone—that accounted for little of the logging companies' profits. Their parents paid their bills. They used the big words they learned in classrooms. I furiously wondered how they could think they were so much better than us.

The investors laughed, slapped each other on the back, and made plans for their logging companies in Latin America. Union activists for indigenous people printed books of songs and poetry in resistance. They didn't want to give up their land. But the union workers were mysteriously shot down on street corners. Old games. Old tricks. Blood soaked into the soil of Oaxaca.

The college students in Olympia eventually put down their chains and protest signs. They moved on to a new fad. They went back to their drum circles and smoked the marijuana that we sold to them—that our parents had grown to feed and clothe us in the sparse new economy. Cota kids got locked up so that college students could get stoned and travel the 101 loop on bicycles. They wore expensive clothing made from hemp. Ate vegan health bars and refused to shower.

They were very proud of their body hair and pale dreadlocks.

The remaining five hundred pairs of northern spotted owl nested in the hollowed-out cavities of old-growth, coniferous timber. They huddled close to the trunks of the Douglas fir. They blended with the bark and the shadows. The big trees were gone. Aggressive barred owls moved into the clear-cuts. A small group of stricken biologists considered the word *defeat*.

Unemployment rates in the logging towns jumped above state and national levels. The economy moved out. Methamphetamines moved in. Logging roads were closed to the public. Meth labs were expensive to clean up. Dealers left the waste behind when they were done. There were abandoned travel trailers and buckets of foul-smelling liquid that could kill. Workers in hazard suits cleaned it up. Rates of domestic violence rose. Families became fractured. The rain poured down relentlessly. But there were some things the water just could not wash away.

Teenagers got pregnant at alarming rates—the highest rates in the nation. But there were no immaculate conceptions in the city of David. Arguments about whose fault it was were lost in the cries of the next generation of hungry babies. The children were talked about in big-city newspaper articles as unwanted vermin. As we were raking her leaves, Mrs. Esworthy told us that kids in timber towns "breed like rabbits." She was tired of her tax dollars going toward our welfare benefits.

Colin watched my body tense as I grew red in the face. It was more salt in more open wounds. He glared warningly. I swallowed and said nothing. I avoided her gaze. She pulled her polar fleece close around her neck. Colin told her we were finished. We walked down the long driveway with our money, stood in a bend of the road, and smoked reservation cigarettes before heading home in silence. I stared at the ground and clenched my jaw in soundless anger that betrayed nothing. It was a long walk back to town.

My father's work boots stood by the door while he slept through the daylight. He still worked swing shift—but not at the mill. My father's work boots stood for something that I wasn't sure about anymore. The security leaked from them. His assurance left along with his pride. His stories were fading. Grandpa passed away from lung cancer. He had breathed in wood dust for too many years. Mother left soon after. Her garden wilted. My blood boiled with the memories of our ancestors. But the stories of the angry prisoners and the deaths of the revolutionary Wobblies were finished. Long ago, the blood had dried and hardened. It was a different color now.

In the new bedroom community, my father was no longer a man, and this hurt him. Hard work didn't matter. He must learn to serve the picky tourists. He took retail and service jobs that didn't pay well or offer health insurance. His strong shoulders withered. He stayed out late into the night trying to make a living. He squinted over his books in the morning. His step became shuffled. He said nothing, over and over and over again. His shame filled up the house on Cota Street. I breathed it in as I slept.

As I got older, I learned to love my father in a different way. His fleeting existence made him transitory. And because of this, perhaps, I loved Jimmy James Blood before I ever saw him. The look of his face or the sound of his voice didn't matter. I liked what happened when the other Cota kids said his name. Their eyes got brighter, and their smiles showed bad teeth. The weariness and indignity backed off their faces. They were proud for a moment. Finally, their very existence was not a burden. A certain power clung to accounts of him. His presence offered a peculiar new feeling to Cota Street. I knew little about him. His reality eluded me. He was from Angel Road back in the hills. He dropped out of school long ago. He was not reluctant. He wore fourteen-eye oxblood boots.

I finally saw him on a summer night—those boots planted

with firm arrogance on the pavement in a dying, industrial town. He stood in the parking lot of the All Night Diner. He looked me in the eye and nodded an affirmation: *Yes. It is true. All of it.* Of course it would be the Fighter Boy from the playground so long ago. Grown up and smirking. He remembered everything. An ocean of writhing, living blood surged between us. It enveloped the parking lot. It discolored the moon. This time the wind did not steal his words from me. Our intention lay naked and squalling in bright red newborn blood. It was dangerous and confusing. But there was no choice.

We were fighters. We were born for it . . . Jimmy James Blood had a whole crew. And a shaved head.

4

FOURTEEN-EYE OXBLOODS

Later (after Annie died). After Brady rolled his Galaxie and Duane burned down the I.W.A. building, I left and took the boots with me.

The fourteen-eye oxbloods were left over from a time that was growing indistinct and far away—a time when Jimmy James could strut into just about any place downtown and everyone turned to watch. The boots were from the time when all us Cota kids knew everything. We held our futures in our laps. They were lean pieces of raw meat hanging tenaciously on to bones and cartilage. We took bites cautiously. We chewed warily. We babied rotten molars and poked out elbows to protect our little portion. We savored the taste of blood in our mouths—the flavor of our destinies.

The fourteen-eye oxbloods were scuffed and muddy and covered in elk blood. I couldn't stand to think of leaving them in the closet and having them found—unpolished. They would be too big of a prize for the Cota kids. Colin let every one of those rats inside the front door. They filled the empty rooms with loud music and cigarette smoke. They stole everything they could while Colin closed his eyes, tilted his head back, and got high. He didn't care much about who was around or what they did. He paid attention to his alcohol, his needles, and global politics. He sighed and let everything go. His black hair grew long and curled at the ends. His black Irish blue eyes were vague and red-rimmed. His body detached. He was nineteen. It was finally too much for him.

I was afraid the Cota kids might take the oxblood boots and use them in a black magic spell. I was afraid they might take them and wear them and spoil everything. They would mock their old leader. They would burn the boots in an angry ceremony—all their respect turning to disappointment and loss. I didn't want the Cota kids to own a piece of anything from that time: the time that was growing hazy in my mind—the time when Jimmy James could walk with such a proud posture of freedom.

I wanted to have the fourteen-eye oxbloods near me—to be able to touch them. I needed the comfort of the leather that had molded to the contours of his ankles. I yearned for the knowledge of how he walked: straightforward and solid—as if he were ready to die for what he believed in.

I tossed the boots in the back of my pickup. I slid my suitcase in over top. The boots scraped along the metal of the bed and nestled into a corner. I bit my lip to keep the tears from coming. The taste of blood reminded me I was alive.

In the house, I stared at the ceiling of the bathroom after I brushed my teeth. The Sheetrock was crumbling in spots. There was a pull-down ladder above me. It allowed access to the crawl space where Colin and I once hid with a fifth of gin. There was a broken window at the end of the crawl space. Colin had kicked the glass out joyously. He'd been drunk and having a fit. "We'll find our *own* way," he'd told me proudly. He'd kicked his boot through the glass to prove he would swallow his future whole— the blood and raw muscle would settle into his hot belly.

I remembered that day. We had clung to a sick euphoria from the cheap liquor.

Crouching in the hot crawl space, Colin had turned to me and grinned. And before I could stop him, he'd jumped through the broken glass and out the window. I'd screamed his name drunkenly and crawled on my belly toward the light of the window. The piney gin odor had curdled in my nostrils. I had peered over the windowsill and expected to see him sprawled out and broken-legged at the bottom. But he'd been laughing and stomping his feet on the broken glass. And yelling for me to follow. I'd glared at him and stayed put.

For a few months, the crawl space was a good hangout. On black nights we stared out at the stars together—shoulder to shoulder out the broken window. Before Mother left, we slept outside to get away from the house on Cota Street—the stress and despair that made our throats close up. We put bottles of beer into our coat pockets and walked to the park. We slapped at mosquitoes. Back then we still wondered what would happen to us. Back then I still wondered what Colin had meant by "our own way."

But now, after everything, I didn't think about what was to come. I threw my toothbrush into my canvas backpack. I woke my bewildered father. I told him I'd be back. He looked at me as if I were speaking to him across a great distance of wilderness filled with a thick, swirling, gray fog. I didn't say I loved him. Neither of us put words to our thoughts—they were too fluttery and numerous.

I walked numbly on the dirt path through the front yard. More car parts would soon nestle inside the moldy picket fence that had fallen inward. Colin would set them there. The grass would grow through them.

I knew that as my father watched me drive away he wouldn't be able to stop thinking about Mother leaving the same way: hurriedly, distractedly, and with assurance.

That day I left the house on Cota Street. I left Colin's broken window, our battered acoustic guitar, and a shelf of priceless records. I packed nothing but a few clothes and notebooks. I filled my truck suddenly and with little thought toward the future. I left with strong shoulders, healthy skin, freckles, and tan lines. I was youth and versatility. I was wisdom and tenacity. I was smiling and sobbing. I was leaving. I didn't really feel alive.

I drove through Eastern Washington with a weight resting on my chest—a cloth bag filled with fishing lead. I drove through Idaho with a tense knot between my shoulder blades. My muscles were granite. I tried rubbing at the anxiety with my fingertips. It wouldn't go away.

In Montana, the sun went down. I was alone, and it was dark, and those big long hills rolled on and on into forever. There was a prairie fire—the tall grass was burning. Black smoke hovered in the night sky. The hills loomed on both sides of the interstate. Glowing orange patches like hell seeped up through the earth to capture me. The full moon kept watch. The gloomy smoke and the glow from the fire made a dense screen between its light and my truck. The smoke was tinged with shadows—burnt and black around the edges. I did not hide from the moon. I drove faster. It was big and like a ghost. It called to me. I took my eyes away from the snaking asphalt to stare.

The smoke drifted in through the cracks in my truck. It was hot—acrid hotness like leaning over glowing coals with your whole body. I took my shirt off because I couldn't stand it anymore. It was lonely on the interstate. Nobody could see me.

I turned around to make sure the boots were still with me. I saw my backpack with a blanket strapped to it. My box of sketchbooks. Jimmy James's camping mat, and my jacket. The smoke and the shadows softened them. My things made dark, lumpy hills like mima mounds at night. I didn't see the boots in my swift glance, and my heart jumped recklessly. I stuck my hand through the open window behind my head and felt around. My fingertips found the warm leather. I sighed with relief.

My radio became quiet somewhere east of the Rocky Mountains. It had trouble picking up a signal. I viewed the miles of highway that I hadn't driven yet. My fancies hummed and swam along Interstate 90. I tried not to become hypnotized by the white line at the edge of the interstate.

I thought about Jimmy James. If everything hadn't happened, he would have been with me. I thought about how firmly he touched my skin. I remembered when he squeezed my arm for the last time. Even though it had been weeks, I still sensed it— each fingertip had left a message on my body. I wondered what he was doing—if the place he was sleeping was comfortable, if the food was making him sick. I hoped he could feel fresh air on his face. I hoped that he knew just what he was going to do and say and where we were going to go when it was all over. If I concentrated hard enough, I could feel his strong, beautiful soul far away and living in some distant space apart from the dim solitude of Montana at midnight.

But he was imprisoned in a cold, dark place with cement walls, and we both heard the sad sounds of our own hopeless thoughts. I inhaled sharply and crazily. I gripped the steering wheel madly.

I tried not to think about Timothy sleeping soundly with a round belly. His little coughs from the cold he was getting over. I tried not to think about his soft skin or his little limbs—the way he curled against my body when he slept. His toys were all packed up. Nadine's strong arms had held him firmly. He'd left screaming for his father. He'd looked at me in terror over Nadine's shoulder—wanting me to make it all better. Nadine was telling him that everything would be okay.

As I looked through my windshield my headlights illuminated the dry, smoky night air. I thought about how wrong Nadine was. I wished for unrealistic possibilities. I wanted everything back: dreams filled with loyalty, luck, and promises. My life was now complicated. Each thought of what came next was filled with the torment of long stretches of empty time and the fear of my hometown.

My body needed Jimmy James. His touch seared all the way through to my bones. Each touch after would pale in comparison. For the rest of my life.

I knew he was there with me in my strange, lonely, wakeful dreams that night. I carried him into the early, big-sky morning along with his boots. He was with me whether I liked it or not. It was beyond my control. I couldn't change my connection to him any more than I could change who my father was or the street where I grew up. I coughed and didn't know what was next.

I was getting farther and farther away. I would soon forget everything. I would be back when all the smoke cleared—when there was nothing but the ashes of what was—the words we held in and the sharp white of Annie's bones in the sawdust-dirt. Jimmy James would be free then, and so would I.

He'd said to *lay low* for a while. He'd written me a note on a yellow piece of paper. So I was lying as low as I could. I would lay so low even my intentions would be lost. I would forget why I was alone. I would forget what his hands felt like. Jimmy James and all the confusion that came along with him would soon become a dream—a fantasy with a shaved head, black Levi's, tattoos, and a vague recollection of muffled thumping noises—rib-cracking methodical violence. The insistent pull of his fingertips would have to stay in the background. I would temporarily lose the memory of how his boots sounded on concrete. The scream that I kept hearing would grow soft and then quiet. The fear would be in the background. I would keep driving shirtless through the fire in Montana—hauling my haphazardly packed bags. And a pair of fourteen-eye oxbloods.

5

ALL TEARS FLOW HOME

My grandparents waited for me at their apartment in Billings, Montana. They waited until they fell asleep on the couch with the television flashing blue lights across their faces. They turned the porch light on after they woke up, noticed I wasn't there yet, and became worried. The light was glowing hopefully in the pink morning light when I finally arrived.

Grandpa came out in his sleeping clothes to greet me. His smile was too full of painful, unconditional love. He walked like Colin used to. His arms were open wide. His hands were rough calluses. His old truck sat in the parking lot with a 4-SALE sign.

I didn't want them to call Mother. I could handle only one devastating thing at a time. Grandma gently told me about Mother's new boyfriend. That I now looked just like her. It was my blond hair. I shook my head. I couldn't swallow it all yet. Even though I was my mother's daughter she had borne me an O'Neel. Tattooed it into my being the day she left.

I slept awkwardly and woke often to the sounds of traffic. The sunlight streamed through the curtains over the small window. My body was not ready for peaceful sleep. My troubles would follow me and destroy everyone I loved. I knew I was a fraud—an imposter with nervous energy. I tossed and turned. I was in trouble. I could gauge my spirit clearly—it had been roaming transparently in angry tempests. I was unable to hide my short fuse and anxiety. I was a wild mustang stabbing at the future with fierce forelegs. I was a bruised teenager who was all alone. I was a solitary fighter. Jimmy James was gone—the loss of him crippled me in ways I never wanted to know about. I tried not to think about it. I needed rest and sustenance. My body felt bent in half as if I were a blade of grass, and my pain was a strong wind. But I could not sleep. Not for the life of me.

I got up around dinnertime. Grandma's quilts were folded against the wall. Her sewing machine with spools of thread and bits of fabric stood beside it. Grandma cooked dinner. The smell of her food made hot tears gather. She always cooked a lot. She was used to feeding more than one family during harvest—when all the farm people gathered together to help each other. All her favorite recipes were quadrupled in the margins of her cookbooks. It was Wednesday.

Jimmy James worked late on Wednesday. I should have been cooking dinner for Timothy—placing his tiny portions on his blue plastic plate, trying to get him to eat with a spoon, watching the mashed potatoes squeeze out of his small fists. Laughing in spite of myself. Picking him up and dancing to Ella Fitzgerald in our small apartment.

I told my grandparents I had to leave soon. I couldn't sit at the table with them and chew my food. I couldn't talk. I knew Grandma would try to coax me to call Mother. She wanted me to stay. But I couldn't explain it all to them. I didn't want to involve my family who had already been through so much. I had too many things I had to take care of—too much distance to travel. I would not be able to rest until there were wide-open spaces between my family and me—between Jimmy James and the cement walls. My burdens weighed heavily. Grandma nodded her head in a way that hurt worse. Her aging body had absorbed enough pain. She understood. There would be more troubles to come.

I stayed on I-90 as I drove through the warm manure odor of Wyoming and South Dakota. I slept uneasily in a rest stop near Sioux Falls. I was on the border of South Dakota and Iowa. It was a town with good energy and a bad smell. I ate hash browns and sunny-side up eggs at a greasy spoon where the waitress refilled my coffee cup habitually to soothe her nerves.

The temperature was rising. I spent two dollars on a pair of leather sandals in Kansas City. I used my pocketknife to cut a pair of jeans into shorts. I tried to relax my jaw. The first freeway sign I saw for St. Louis was broken in two. It read ST. LO. When I entered the city I looked around me with as much interest as I could muster. I listened to every sound. I smelled all that I could smell. It was late August, molten hot, the air like boiling oil on my rain-soaked Washington skin. My body resented the bright, humid summer. I was used to darkness and mildew.

In the city of David it could rain a hundred inches a year. It rained for weeks on end.

When I was a kid, Cota Street scoffed at our huddled figures. Squatters came in from the woods. The line at the homeless shelter grew longer. The liquor store was busier. Crowds gathered outside of the AA meetinghouse. Everything took longer in the rain. Us Cota kids laughed instead of crying. We looked up into the dark sky. We shouted curse words and threw punches in vicious fights.

I crossed the Mississippi and entered East St. Louis. The low-fuel warning light lit up in my truck. I parked and walked until the wind whipped my hair and the slow-moving dark water was before me. I'd barely slept in three days. I was Wesley Everest standing on the bank of the Skookumchuck. With blood on my hands. With mud on my boots. With nothing between death and a river. There was water and fear. My blood went cold. It turned to ice in my veins.

I walked to a pay phone and tried to think of who to call. Across the street, three older men holding large bottles of liquor hidden in brown paper bags were passing around a lumpy blunt. They stared at me from their street corner. The shock was wearing off. I didn't have anywhere to go. I didn't have any money.

East St. Louis stared me down.

The receiver demanded that I make a decision. It clicked. I looked at the pay phone with no shelter—all by itself out on the dirty corner with nothing but two teenagers examining a broken radio, arguing about how to fix it. The broken glass from beer and liquor bottles reflected the sun that was getting lower in the sky. The heat seemed to fluctuate; it gathered around my head.

I wanted a place to stay: a private place to sleep, a stove to cook a meal on. I felt the parking lot spinning loosely and crazily. It was hot. I felt sick and dizzy and young and stupid.

I yelled, "Goddamnit!" at no one. The teenagers took off running down an alley where the garbage was cooking in blue metal bins. I slammed the receiver down angrily. The broken radio skidded into the street and rested in the indentation of a sewer drain. I got in my truck and sat there, thinking. I sighed and got out. I dialed the phone number of the only one who was in as deeply as me.

"Where the *hell* have you been?" Brady Robbins demanded when he heard my voice. "Your dad said you left! Nobody's *seen* you!" His voice rose in searing pain. The girl he loved was gone. Three weeks ago, he'd seen his best friend handcuffed and wavering in and out of consciousness. Three weeks ago, he'd leaned against me in stricken silence as the rain drowned us, and we said nothing.

Brady gave me five hundred dollars. He deposited the money into my bank account. It was half a month's pay for him. He shushed me when I worried out loud. "My best friend will pay me back when he's out and can get work." I inhaled sharply. Brady was delusional. He floated in cloudy, marginalized pain. Annie was gone. There had been no funeral. Everyone was broke. Her soul was stuck in purgatory.

I drove until I found a quiet parking lot to sleep in. I sang Dead Boys songs to myself.

Dark clouds moved in overhead. The sky growled with thunder. I watched as lightning lit up the sky. The summer night was murky and the land was flat. I could see far into the distance. There were no mountains with forests of Sitka spruce around their bases. There were no jagged peaks covered in glistening white ice. There were no clear-cuts where small, new-green Douglas fir hurried to populate the naked brown earth. I did not hear logging trucks. There were no sharp cliffs where angry restless seawater hammered rocks relentlessly. The narrow, fast rivers that swallowed and gulped and raged were a memory that was leaving me. I was surrounded by old land that was once on the edge of an ancient glacier. The hemlock and western red cedar did not crouch here. There was no fog—no steam from the tidewater mill. There was flat, baked, brown land. There were buildings much older and wiser than me. Fat, warm droplets of water splattered my skin. I watched the rain fill up the parking lot and drain the dust from my dented, white Ford. Warm Illinois rain—I had never touched or seen or tasted warm rain.

I remembered how Colin and I used to watch storms. We'd stop what we were doing, tell the Cota kids to shut up or get out. Our sentences would hang in the air—unfinished. We would watch the forks of light explode in the sky and forget everything else.

Colin would have been impressed by the storm in Illinois. He would have raised his arms to the sky and encouraged me to run out into the rain with him. He would have stomped, splashed, and grinned in the swirling rivers of dirty, agitated water.

But he was back in David—strung out.

And I was alone in East St. Louis sleeping in a parking lot. I didn't get out of my truck. I was afraid. I didn't feel eighteen. I felt like a very old woman with a body that remembered strain. All I could offer the murky evening was a blandly wistful stare. They'd taken Jimmy James away. He'd been stumbling blindly and covered in blood. He couldn't hold me in the warm rain. I couldn't watch his biceps flex underneath his tattoos. I slept fitfully and warily.

In the morning I ate a salty breakfast at a diner. I brushed my teeth in the bathroom. I tipped the waitress in change. "It's all I got," I apologized. She pushed the coins back at me firmly.

"Chile', you keep them coins fo' y'self!" she told me. "You look like you need 'em a *whole* lot more 'n me."

I realized that my eyes must have looked hungry, that she could see my yellowing bruises. She shook her head and said something about me being in a *heap o' trouble* as she walked away. She said her words gently and lowly. She made the cook give me extra hash browns in a white, Styrofoam to-go container. She squeezed my shoulder like a strong grandmother. My muscles relaxed where she touched me. She swept the floor and sang hymns to herself.

I used the coins to make a few phone calls, and got an apartment in the Southside of St. Louis. I hoped it would have a place to sit in the shade. I drove and then climbed the musty stairs to the very top of the brick building called Ivanhoe. The steps were wooden and built to last. The walls were tiled. I fumbled to unlock the door. The apartment had no refrigerator or air conditioning. It smelled like dogs. I had never felt so tired. There was an oak tree in front. The cicadas lost in its branches screamed out their indignation of the heat. I opened up every window that wasn't painted shut. I felt very lucky.

The front door had four locks. I slid and clicked them into place when I stepped inside. They made me feel four times as safe. There was a wilted marijuana plant in a pot outside the kitchen door. I sat beside it on the fire escape with a sketchbook. I drew the different things I saw. I examined the backs of the buildings. The parked cars looked strange and my neighbors sullen. Hot breezes swept my hair across my sweating forehead.

I slept on Jimmy James's camping mattress that night. It smelled of wood smoke and sweat. I tried to dream of him but the heat closed in on me. Hot moisture filled every movement and breath. I wet towels in the sink and covered my body. I listened to the street noises. Dogs barked. People yelled at one another. Sirens screamed unmercifully.

I tried to muffle my sobs into the folded sweatshirt I was using as a pillow. But the safety of the four walls let the tears come out. It was too much. I added to the noises outside. I cried and beat my fists against the hardwood floor. My skin cracked open over my bones. Blood dried on my knuckles. My movement left streaks in the dust.

I was left with a shaky, wrung-out feeling. And shame.

I put clothes on and walked down Lafayette until I found a gas station. I bought a pack of cigarettes with four crumpled dollar bills. The girl working slid them to me in a metal tray. She watched me listlessly through the bulletproof glass. She scolded the drunk man behind me to stop crowding my space. He stopped leaning against me. He stopped asking for my number.

I smoked in the dark in my new apartment. My mind drew shapes on the blank walls. They were colored with the hues of my memory.

I tried to be stronger than I had been before. I tried to believe that inside those cement walls, Jimmy James was still proud. And that soon I would feel his chest under my cheek. I remembered simple things: Like Timothy playing in the bedroom after dinner while Jimmy James washed the dishes and talked animatedly. And how I sat at the table and drew wildflowers. And how every so often Timothy would miss us and run into the kitchen to earnestly show us his toys. Things like that.

I tried to dry the new flow of hot saltwater down my cheeks. Because I knew that all my tears would flow back home. I knew Colin wouldn't speak to me if I called. He would hide in a deep, undisturbed silence. He wouldn't want to hear my voice. During my last days home, Colin felt the pain coming out of my body. He knew about my bruises without me telling him. I couldn't hide from my brother—my worries filled the space in between us.

We were white trash, and white trash are wrong a lot.

It was bigger than us now. Jimmy James was locked up downtown. The Cota kids had stopped believing. Colin knew the whole story without me telling him. New bruises appeared where the old ones yellowed. He threw rocks at parked cop cars. He stayed out late drinking. He avoided looking me in the eye. He slept on the couch.

I took good care of the fourteen-eye oxblood boots in my new apartment. I oiled them with black polish on Sunday. I stared at the ceiling and let my bruises heal. I drew pictures on my walls with a pencil. The shapes kept developing scary shadows. There were faces with eyes swollen shut, bloody teeth, and a recently fired .45—a 1911 with a pearl pistol grip. Scattered across the images were bullet casings—each one of them with invisible, devastating fingerprints.

6

WHEN MOTHER LEFT

The Cota Street house was next to the railroad tracks. We could hear the rumbling and the sound of the long, lonely whistles all night. The trains carried the big logs into the mill. We watched the loads of cut lumber come out. Sometimes, Colin and I sat on the back porch and snuck cigarettes with our cousin Daemon. We strained our ears to listen to the music from the taverns—varied forms of off-tune karaoke singing—drums and bass from live bands.

Mother could never find it in her heart to turn Daemon away. He was her nephew but more than that. She had raised him since he was a little baby.

He visited during hard times. He talked about his heartache in drunken slurs—lost love—bad luck—things that just didn't come easily. He chain-smoked and drank cheap beer from tall cans. He slept on our couch. His laughter shook the walls. He always had presents for me and Colin. He never asked for much. He was happy with food and a blanket. Mother let us listen to his stories—it was how he earned his keep. She huddled close to the woodstove with her books and her cat while he entertained us. She shivered in the cold wind that blew through the cracks in the walls. The house on Cota Street was old and cheaply built. It made her feel like she was back in the hills.

Daemon's visits reminded her of the two-room cabin she grew up in—the chinking between the logs—the unfinished wood—the yard without flowers and the seven children she helped raise. It wasn't that she hated the memory of that cabin so much. What she hated was how hard it was to make that cabin disappear at will. What she hated was how that cabin looked to other people—how they saw it without knowing about the quilts and Christmas presents and joy and hardship and love. She worked hard to sharpen her accent—to forget the words that weren't in dictionaries.

Colin and I worked odd jobs with Daemon. We cut firewood on state land. We picked blackberries, blueberries, and huckleberries that we froze to eat later. We picked brush and mushrooms for quick cash and cut boughs during the holiday season. We got rides with Dad when he went to visit Granny O'Neel. We took trips to Aberdeen and Elma with our O'Neel cousins. We wore steel-toe boots and went to live music shows. We were shameless and bold and alive.

Daemon never stayed long. He drifted off to see other family in California or Oregon or British Columbia. He slung his backpack over his shoulder, revved his motorcycle before waving good-bye. He sped off when the train whistle blew. We all felt suddenly restless, and didn't blame him for leaving.

Mima never sat on the back porch with us. She didn't work odd jobs or go to shows. She was tough in her own way. Her eyes grew tired from reading by the light of kerosene lanterns. She developed splitting headaches and rubbed at her temples in Dad's easy chair.

Mother started to not like Cota Street—living so close to the train tracks got to her after a while. It was worse after her parents moved to Montana. Daemon still came sporadically. But Mother started to stare a lot. She looked out the old, single-pane windows with nothing on her face. She thought her sad thoughts. I wanted to shake her. I wanted to bring her back because she was a thousand miles away. She saw terrible things out that window—things that weren't the neighbor's brightly colored toys getting wet and moldy on their mud and crabgrass lawn. The things she saw were bigger than all of us—they couldn't be fixed. Sometimes she was sad for long periods. When she stared out the window with no answers, she made a choice—a dark and hopeless one. I knew she wanted to leave. She stopped sleeping at night toward the end. She had a strained look on her face. She waited. One Friday, Colin and I waited up with her. We all waited for Dad to come home.

Dad was tired when he walked in the door that last night Mother was home. It was midnight. His auburn beard was listless. His union meeting had depressed him. He took off his tattered wool jacket. He felt worn-out. He wanted to drink his glass of whiskey and be alone for a few hours—nurse his personal wounds.

But we'd been up waiting for a long time. We tried to show him things. But Dad didn't want to talk. He didn't want to come and see the castle Colin had built out of cards. Or the picture of Bob Dylan that I'd drawn on newsprint. Our excitement turned to disappointment. Dad wasn't impressed. My lower lip pouted out. We acted up. Colin and I argued loudly. Mima screamed at us that she had to "get *up* in the morning!" Mother cried. She accused Dad of things: seeing other women, not loving her. She wanted him to hold her. He didn't know if he still could.

Dad talked of giving up his job at the mill and moving back to the swamp—living off the land like they'd done before they had us kids. Before they got married. He wanted to help Granny out now that his father was dead. He said she was getting older. It was a personal conversation. But the house was small. Colin and I were listening. We piped up that we'd help feed the chickens and milk the goats.

Mother didn't like that we'd been listening. She told us to go outside. We stood on the back porch and peered in at them through the window. The single-pane glass let us hear everything. She told Dad the whole idea was stupid. She didn't want her kids to be "hillbillies with no future." She reminded him that we would never, not in a million years, be able to sell our house on Cota Street. Tourists were the only ones who bought houses. And none of them wanted to live next to "Cota kids and immigrants along the railroad tracks."

Dad spoke gently. He said Granny would let us build our own cabin in her little valley. Mother rolled her eyes. She reminded him that we'd have to pay for permits and our savings were almost drained. School buses didn't go out that far. Not even the rural routes. The roads closed down "*all* winter long!" She didn't want to live with temperamental Granny. She wanted us to make it on our own. She didn't want Colin and me spending any more time with our O'Neel cousins. She said, "We don't even have a damn *car*!"

Dad told her Colin and I could learn on our own—from books like he had. His nieces and nephews were not bad people— just a little rough.

Colin and I yelled in excitement that we didn't *want* to go to school. We didn't *like* classrooms. The kids at junior high were snobby. We knew we could chop firewood, raise rabbits, and pump water. We knew we could help Dad fix cars for money.

"I could bake bread!" I added.

"I could hunt with my shotgun!" Colin said.

We had forgotten we were spying. Mother came close to the window with her hands balled up in fists. We knew we were in for it. She was so mad her knees and elbows shook. "Go to your rooms!" she screamed at us through the window. But Colin slept on the couch. And Mima didn't want me in the bedroom while she was trying to sleep. We stayed where we were.

Mother threw Dad's worn-out work boots at him. One by one. He tried to keep it all together. In frantic bursts he talked about relaxing. Fixing his truck. Going fishing like they used to. They could get a few hens and grow potatoes. His words excited Colin and me. We smelled fish crackling in cast iron. We felt the deep heat of an open fire—freedom and wilderness.

Mima finally got out of bed and asked what all the yelling was about. She told Dad she would *never* go back to the family land in the swamp. She reminded him curtly that soon enough there would be no more woods to escape to. Granny would have to come live with *us*. "You don't know *anything*!" she told Dad. She stared smoothly at him—challenged his very existence. She had dark circles under her eyes. She was in her pajamas—short cotton pants and a tank top. "You're uneducated and stubborn," she said pointedly. She was past the point of no return. Her nipples poked angrily against her shirt. "You're just like *Granny*!" She lost her cool and went after him with her pointer finger. She was poking at his chest and yelling in his face. She was almost as tall as him. Long and tall and thin and redheaded. "I don't know if you've *noticed*, but *O'Neels* are all *trash*!"

The word *trash* hit Colin and me like a punch to the gut. Dad stared at his painting of a ship he had hung carefully on the wall. His shoulders wilted. I couldn't see his face. I thought about how he camped for days bringing only a knife and a frying pan. I thought about him being so good-looking in the driveway working on his truck. *Trash?* Colin and I looked at each other in the square of yellow light from the window. Dad didn't say a word. The world seemed suddenly unstable. Dad told Mima to go to bed and get some sleep. She gritted her teeth and looked down her nose at him before stalking away.

Mother was sobbing desolately—she'd had a lot of wine. I leaned against the wooden windowsill outside and inhaled sharply.

Colin gripped my arm hard and pulled me away from the house. He had the rest of Mother's wine stashed in his jacket. After sitting down on the railroad tracks and taking a long swallow I calmed down. We decided it was too cold to sleep in the park. We walked up to Monique Potter's instead.

Monique was getting a tattoo in her living room. Her mom worked graveyard. Monique was happy to see us. She smoked all her pot with us and made chocolate cake when her tattoo was done. Colin laughed at Monique's impersonation of the president telling Gulf War veterans they weren't really sick. I fell asleep on the couch.

We went back to Cota Street in the morning. Mother was gone. Mima was packing. Dad was sleeping.

The next couple of days Dad looked bewildered—without a trace of understanding—just a big, dark guilt of things that neither of us could comprehend.

Mima stuck around to finish high school. But she didn't live with us. She stayed with a church family. "It's closer to the high school, and I can have my own room," she explained.

Colin and I celebrated his fourteenth birthday by staying home from school and listening to radio news shows in the kitchen. We made Jell-O with whipped cream and listened to a journalist who said US tanks were in Baghdad, unemployed men walked the streets of Iraq, and teenage boys were starting militias. We listened to a journalist who tried to explain "Seattle grunge music" as a political movement. He called it "the voice of a generation." We thought that was silly. Because we knew that grunge was the sound of a screaming saw blade, a spawning salmon flicking gravel. It looked like a clear-cut. And if you cracked grunge open, you would find a moldy fifth-wheel trailer inside.

A week later, we decided to go to one of Mima's soccer games. Colin had a green mohawk. I shaved my head and drew a black star on my scalp. Dad was asleep when we left. We'd been quiet all morning, and we were sick of being good. Colin brought his boom box and his Dropkick Murphys tape. I had a pack of stale cigarettes in my back pocket. I smoked one on the way up the hill just to bother Colin. He told me I was too young—tried to swipe it out of my hand. His fist hit the live cherry. It burned a round welt into his skin. He didn't flinch. I thought it was a badass thing for him to do: *not flinch.* I tried to burn my own arm to see how bad it hurt. I flinched. "You can only burn yourself in places where you have *calluses*," Colin explained. I listened carefully. I knew Colin was smarter than me.

We sat down quietly when we got to the soccer field. We were late. The sun was out. We spread our sweatshirts down on the grass and sat on them. We put the silent boom box in front of us. Colin sipped from his water bottle filled with vodka and grape soda. He drank it fast so it wouldn't get warm. He gave me a few sips. We had all the good intentions in the world.

Ratboy Evans walked by and saw us sitting in the sun. We called him Ratboy because he had a rattail for a long time after they were popular. He sat down next to us. His combat boots dug into the ground. The smell of his feet mixed with the scent of the cheap military leather. The sun felt hot on my alcohol-warmed face. Ratboy took out his pouch of tobacco and rolled cigarettes. Mima made a goal, and we all cheered. Colin whistled long and loud. He stood up.

"Woo*whee*!" Ratboy Evans yelled even louder, trying to outdo Colin. He stood and clapped his hands, stuck his fingers in his mouth, and whistled. His leftover tobacco fell from his blue jeans and mixed with the carefully fertilized grass of the playing field.

The smoke from the teenage boys drifted down. Parents wrinkled their noses and faked stern coughing fits. I took out my own pack of stale smokes. Ratboy saw me and shoved one of his rolled cigarettes at me. "It's the filters that kill people," he told me. I didn't listen carefully. I knew I was smarter than him.

Colin gave Ratboy his water bottle. Ratboy finished it in one, long drink. His rattail was gone now. He wore his hair slicked back and a black leather jacket. He belched.

Mima slide-tackled illegally. She was carded. We booed raucously. For too long probably. People glared at us. Ratboy and Colin ignored them. Both boys were red-faced and laughing. They good-naturedly shoved each other.

Monique saw us at the soccer field from her house across the street. She came over and offered us beers in her kitchen. We trudged after her across the hot pavement. We walked in front of a car. "WATCH IT!" Ratboy shouted. He yelled it loudly enough so that people from the game turned to stare. It was the church lady Mima was staying with. She'd been driving too fast. We flipped the car off even though it was *us* who had walked in front of it. We flipped off the people from the soccer field who were still staring.

We piled into Monique's dark kitchen and drank the cold beers as fast as we could—sucked down the joint that Ratboy provided. Monique said we had to hurry—she wasn't sure when her mom was getting home from her boyfriend's house. She turned up Peter Tosh on her stereo. I was squished against Ratboy Evans in the tiny kitchen—I felt his hard chest breathing. I smelled his hair oil and all his black leather. I smelled Monique's cheap perfume and her toothpaste breath. I couldn't smell Colin at all because he smelled just like me.

We walked back across the street. The game was just ending.

Spectators were straggling into their vehicles—the soccer kids were drinking red sports drinks from a blue cooler that one of the moms in designer pants had brought. Mima was standing on the sidewalk with our sweatshirts. She was waiting for us. She had her arms crossed and her lips pursed. Her curly red hair was swept up in a high ponytail and her muscled calves were flexed. Her face was flushed. She noticed our bloodshot eyes.

For a moment, I thought she was waiting for us because she won her game and was excited to tell us. I had three one-dollar bills in my right pocket. I wanted to buy her ice cream to celebrate. I stuck my hand in my jeans to make sure the money was still there. The bills curled reassuringly against my thigh.

But Monique and Ratboy knew something was up when they saw Mima standing across the street. Their steps became reticent.

Mima launched our sweatshirts at us one at a time. *"FOR-GET* something?!" Her words were like icy knives in my gut. Colin let his sweatshirt fall to his feet as he looked at our sister levelly. I felt silly for catching mine. So I let it drop from my hand. But it was too late. A car loaded with people inched around us on the street. I wanted to tell Mima that we hadn't really forgotten our sweatshirts—we had left them because we were only gone a minute.

I heard Peter Tosh singing plainly from Monique's house. We'd forgotten to turn the stereo off.

I didn't want my sweatshirt now. I didn't want to have anything to do with it. I stared at the black cotton at my feet. It was covered in rude patches. It offended Mima, who studied so hard. "Did you forget *these*, too?!" She threw all our cigarette butts at us—Colin's, Ratboy's, and mine. She had dug them out of the grass after we pushed them underneath the dirt. I rushed to pick them up. I wanted to tell her that we had thought about it—Ratboy had assured us that since they were "biodegradable" it was okay to leave them in the grass. We should have known better. Both Colin and I were smarter than Ratboy.

I noticed a crowd watching. A group of kids from Mima's youth group and their parents. I looked into their golden faces. I knew the girls' tan lines followed the contours of bathing suits. And mine were in the shape of T-shirts. I saw their clean shorts and brand-name soccer cleats. They were still breathing hard from their heavenly, decent, *civilized* exertion. Not a shaved head among them.

I started to crumble. We were wrong again—kids like me and Colin and Monique and Ratboy were wrong a lot. I was going to cry like a baby. Colin socked my arm hard to make me stop.

I put the cigarette butts in one hand and carried them to a metal trash can. The lid was chained to the fence—flies buzzed around it. I passed Mima and cringed away from her bewildering energy. She stood straight, and it reminded me of her astrological sign: the archer shooting true.

Mima sighed. "Can you guys just *LEAVE*?" She didn't want us there. She didn't want us to drink sports drinks with her soccer friends and their soccer parents or eat ice cream with us in the park. I swallowed hard. I heard Colin saying what Dad said to Mother until she left: "You think your shit don't stink." Colin said it like he was far away—like he wasn't really there. Like he was standing above Mima and looking down from a lofty place.

Mima could never keep her cool for long. Her voice cracked and went high. She told him to "SHUDDUP!"

Colin smiled. He walked cockily inside the fence and re-
trieved his boom box. He looked at every one of the soccer boys
in turn, and they stopped drinking sports drinks and talking
so lightheartedly. They cast wary glances at him—shifted their
weight from foot to foot. They suddenly looked stupid in their
shiny, polyester soccer shirts. Their muscles didn't mean anything. Colin had spent the last month splitting firewood with
Daemon for fifty bucks a cord. He was loud guitars and wasted
lives and spit on pavement. Things they didn't know.

Colin rejoined us and we walked down the sidewalk toward
the steep hill that went back downtown. He stuck his shoulders
forward intensely—glaring uncontrollably at the hill. He tensed
at the vague sounds from the mill and the reverberations of the
train whistle.

Monique said, "What a crazy bitch."

Colin stopped walking to look sternly into her eyes. "Don't
call my sister that."

"Sorry." Monique scratched at the back of her neck—her
snake tattoo that was healing.

"She ain't crazy." Colin took a deep breath. He smiled a small
smile. He pushed Monique playfully. She grabbed on to his arm
and held it—gleaned strength from his boyish, offhand violence.

I looked at the top of the hospital roof where the sun was pink
and setting. After sunset it would grow cold quickly. I wondered
if we could stop at the city park and swing on the swings while we
finally played our Dropkick Murphys tape.

I turned back to look at the soccer field. Mima stood on the
corner but she didn't look so mad anymore. She looked sad and
deflated. Like she was remembering stuff she'd forgotten about:

maybe the Christmas that I knitted mittens in her school colors. Or the famous tantrums Colin used to throw when he was a toddler.

I stopped walking and watched her face that was growing soft in the light of the setting sun. She almost looked like she wanted to come with us. But the church lady she was staying with called to her. She waved. I walked away from my sister. I walked more slowly than the others. I thought about my favorite Radiohead song. I wanted to sing apprehensively to kill the tension. The quickly cooling wind brought cold little droplets of rain.

Colin walked close when I rejoined them. He let his arm touch mine. He elbowed me sharply and quickly. He looked straight ahead innocently as if it were an accident. I kicked him hard with my boot in his calf. He howled and crumpled to the ground. I looked straight ahead innocently as if it were an accident. He limped to his feet and grinned.

He started to whistle. I knew all his whistling songs—his tunes and his patterns. I listened to that and his feet stepping.

I was glad Monique and Ratboy liked us, and we were all together. I understood why Daemon was restless and Mima studied so hard, but I wouldn't leave the house on Cota Street for a long time. I knew we wouldn't really go back to the swamp with Dad. He would stay at the mill. And our lives would take place on Cota Street.

We stopped at the park and listened to our tape. Then Monique brought out Toots and the Maytals. We took our time getting home.

Mima got grants to go along with her scholarship fund. Montana State University welcomed her. She came to say good-bye to us on Cota Street. She brought four of her closest church friends with her. Colin and I huddled on the back porch and listened to her talk to Dad through the window. Mima kept her back straight. Her friends looked around our house curiously. They eyed the swords, hunting bows, and the painting of the ship hanging on the walls. An axe gleamed above the fireplace. A rifle leaned beside the door.

When Mima and her friends left, Dad looked lost. He stared out the window all day. He didn't see the neighbor's yard. He didn't watch the swing set creaking back and forth with the weight of the little girl swinging on it. He was thinking his thoughts and feeling his sadness. His tired hands gripped the chair arms.

I wondered if he was thinking about Mima singing in the shower—how we could hear her all over the house. I figured he was thinking about those things, and those things were wrapped up so tightly in memories of Mother he just couldn't move anymore.

We let him sit there. I brought him one of the corn dogs that Colin and I made for dinner. I put it on a plate with a bright circle of red ketchup. He thanked me but didn't touch it. He told me he would go hunting soon. Finally, after the whole day, he put his face in his hands. He rested there like that for a long time.

Colin and I cleaned the bedroom after Mima left town. We wanted to keep her stuff nice so when she came back she would see how proper we really were. She would see that we hadn't let any of the Cota kids run up in her stuff and steal everything. We took turns practicing how to talk like the church kids. We said *perhaps* and *God's love.* We rolled on the freshly swept floor in sad

fits of laughter. Our mockery was a weapon that protected us—
our mirth was a sharp, bloody sword.

Dad snapped out of his sad thoughts the next morning when
Daemon came. He smiled at the sound of the motorcycle. He
combed his hair and put on a clean shirt. He got to work frying
bacon and eggs for all of us.

Colin and I sat with Daemon on the back porch with the
door open. We heard the sound of Johnny Horton from the radio
in the kitchen. We smelled strong black coffee brewing.

Daemon told us he would stay until we got sick of him. Colin
and I cheered. "That's going to be *never!*" I told him.

Daemon yelled to Dad through the open door that Mother
was weird about some things. That she would come back when
she got over it. But I remembered the look in her eyes when she
stared out the window and saw sad things. I knew somehow that
he was full of it.

I told Daemon that if I ever got married, I would keep my
last name. That I would be an O'Neel until I died. He told me he
already felt sorry for the poor sucker who got roped into marrying
me. He said that a woman as mean as me could take years off
a man's life. Colin whistled happily. Daemon chain-smoked his
cigarettes. He drank cheap beer from a tall can. We all waited for
the sound of the train.

PART 2

7

THE NORTHSIDE

I got a job at a grade school in the Northside of St. Louis.

In the Northside the ghetto flew at me adamantly. I viewed it in a confused haze. The inner city fluttered impatiently—demanded to be seen—insisted that I know it intimately and immediately. I could not concentrate. I could not drown in my own thoughts. The streets stared at me—waiting. The children watched attentively while I struggled.

The stoplights went from green to red and back to yellow in a pattern that had no rhyme or reason. The custodian, Mr. P, told me that crack fiends pulled the wires out of the streetlights so intersections would be dark at night. He said cars were easier to rob that way.

I watched mentally ill people wander the desolate avenues. I wondered about them. They talked to themselves—yelled out obscenities. They were picked up from the rich neighborhoods and loaded into squad cars. They couldn't afford medication or therapy. So they slept fitfully in abandoned buildings. They woke in strange places tortured by their own demons. People in the suburbs forgot about them.

I gave them names. There was Bottle Cap Man, who wore a jacket with metal bottle caps pinned like armor across his shoulders. There was Patti Smith, who was proud, frustrated, and brilliant. There was Mirabella, who wore a torn and dirty sequined gown.

I worried when I didn't catch them in their usual spots. I examined from afar their unmanned stacks of rubble blowing in the wind—the contents of their shopping carts torn to pieces. I wondered what had happened. My mind jumped to awful conclusions.

I watched as Bottle Cap Man crouched in the center of the street—his trench coat flapping in the wind. The tails of his green woolen jacket resembled a dirty cape that might help him fly. He looked like he'd run to that particular spot with the idea of saving someone—only to find that his help was not needed. Or wanted. There was nothing but a chill morning wind and cracked asphalt to greet him. His face held confusion for a moment. He looked like a mistaken superhero. He sprung upright and waved his hands. He screamed silently. He knew he'd made a mistake. The wind and traffic noise blew his words away. I looked at him waiting there. He disappeared behind a garbage truck that did not slow down for him.

The Northside was overflowing with children whose ancestors had been chased there from sundown towns with sticks and rocks. They were forced into the Northside after the rich families moved out—when the pollution from the factories became too much.

The families that now lived on the Northside looked back at their unwritten histories.

The future spread out before them. They knew the truth. They tried not to let their hearts harden irreversibly.

I worked at Meadows Elementary. The trophy case held framed photographs of a much different student body: smiling pale faces all in a row, freshly starched dresses, blond hair, and pigtails tied with ribbons. The pictures were from a much richer time. Long, long ago.

Mr. P caught me staring at the pictures in bewilderment. "Yes, *ma'am*," he answered my silent question. I was startled and turned toward him. "Used to be a *white* school." He raised his eyebrows at me and kept walking slowly down the glowing, hardwood floor. He pushed his cart filled with squeegees, paper towels, garbage bags, and a bottle of bleach. He whistled a cheerful tune. His eyes sparkled in amusement.

The children at Meadows told me things. They imagined their stories as ordinary. They did not anticipate that my brain would churn each time they spoke. I confiscated their words hungrily. I coaxed them to share more. Their eyes grew round with excitement. They carefully explained the events of their lives. I kept my face grave. I nodded seriously. They dove into heavy details without hesitation. I learned about their lives. I imagined their situations. I tried to make sense of it all, and drew half-baked conclusions that I mulled over late at night. In turn they studied my gestures and got to know my speech patterns. They asked startling personal questions about why my hair was so straight, my eyes and blood so blue, and my words so soft and stumbling.

A fifth grader named Diamond held my hand. She told me I was her "play momma." Every confidence was precious. Each stare was a mesmerizing, painful experience. I was being patiently judged, and I knew it. I could not blame the children. They had seen too many things. I tried not to misinterpret. I failed often. It was hard to trust. It was hard for all of us.

Meadows smelled like old wood and rats. The hardwood floors were polished to a high gloss. The principal introduced himself to me and the other new girl—Trinise. He proudly explained how important that floor was. He told us that Meadows was famous for it shining so brightly, so vibrantly. I tried to tread lightly on it as if it were something more than wood—something special and secret—perhaps made of gold.

I listened to the teachers discipline harshly. I heard them yell over the large groups of young people. Each voice was straining to be heard.

It was hard. It would only get harder.

Things were overlooked at Meadows Elementary—minor details that demoralized. Little things slipped in between the cracks: spoiled food was delivered at lunchtime, the lack of air conditioning kept us all sweating, fresh vegetables were rare, there was little time for drawing class, too few funds for sports equipment or music lessons, standardized testing took up important time, the district was watching for signs of failure, the fear of losing accreditation loomed, the tap water tasted like turpentine, the mice were out of control, the teachers were overworked. They encountered one problem after another. They were exhausted.

My head was tired after long days at Meadows. I came home with aching temples. I was relieved to fall into my bed at night. I experienced black sleep without dreams. I woke to my alarm and hot mornings. I did not think about anything.

At Meadows Elementary Trinise and I were hall monitors, lunchroom monitors, and playground monitors. We monitored and we monitored.

I watched the fights during recess. Girls fought boys, little kids fought big kids, brothers fought sisters, and cousins spit and cussed at one another. I secretly didn't find the fights as alarming as I was supposed to. I knew that the children should keep practicing—that there would be a lot more surprise punches thrown. I wanted them to be able to defend themselves against their many enemies who wore different types of uniforms.

I kept the teenaged boys from the neighborhood off the basketball nets. They jeered and flirted. They walked away and looked back at me.

Mrs. Halls told me not to hug the children during recess—they would not respect me if I did. I let them do it anyway. I wondered how I could say no. Their hot foreheads rubbed sweat on my T-shirts. I secretly needed their fierce embraces. Trinise jumped rope with the older girls. I watched her. She asked if I wanted to join in. I turned the ropes for them awhile. But I would not go into the center. I pictured the ropes smacking my head. I was too big for kids' games.

Mrs. Halls taught fifth grade. She was old and thin. She was hard lines. Narrow glasses perched on her nose. A scowl occupied her face. Her hair was pulled back tightly. Little wisps of white escaped and framed her face. I imagined that she woke at 5 a.m. each morning. She was never late. Mrs. Halls was six feet tall. She was like a stone statue, a skyscraper, or a sturdy oak tree. She had long, bony arms. They did not hug the children. She glared down her nose.

On my first day her eyes estimated me unabashedly from

behind her square glasses. Her upper lip was stiff. Her eyes were cold. I wanted her to smile at me or nod her head. But I knew I would have to earn those things. It was hard to trust. We both had our fingers on our triggers.

Mrs. Halls was a giant spider crouched behind her desk. Three hundred miles stood between us. I crossed and uncrossed my arms nervously. Her back was ramrod straight. I said nothing. She firmly told me the rules: I was to be referred to by my last name, *Ms. O'Neel,* I was to greet her in the mornings, and I was to be polite. I held my hillbilly tongue.

I watched the children in Mrs. Halls's classroom, and they watched me. I set my notebook on the kid-size table. I looked at the books on the shelf beside me. I watched two young men cross the street and yell to one another. American cars drove by. The sunshine burned up the tired, old neighborhood.

I sketched some of the students—concentrated on faces and eyebrows—the way sunlight reflected off dark skin. I wished that I had colored pencils to re-create the warm tones—brown with hints of red and yellow, shading with purple and blue.

Mrs. Halls scowled when she caught me drawing (I was supposed to be paying attention). My drawings were distracting the students. The children had begun to pose.

I put my notebook away and smiled. She glared back. I sighed, stretched my back, and tried to sit up straight.

Mr. P told me Mrs. Halls did not want me in her classroom. He said I was another injustice put upon her by the state of Missouri. Instead of giving her school district adequate supplies, they gave her me: an eighteen-year-old with a GED who drew pictures. He told me things I had not known: Mrs. Halls was fifty-six years old, Mrs. Halls had a PhD, Mrs. Halls was a longtime member of the Black Panther Party, Mrs. Halls could have gone somewhere else to work—taught at a university. But she came back to the Northside where she grew up.

I had a feeling Mrs. Halls wanted something more than me. She wanted the whole machine to crumble—to stop eating her children.

I met Marvin in the hallway. He was another young tutor. He was supposed to train Trinise and me. When he saw me, he put his hand up as if he were hailing a cab. His eyes showed a moment of surprise. He wore a dress shirt, khaki pants, and shiny shoes. His mouth remained stuck open in shock. He thrust his hand toward me. I shook it and put my head to the side. I crossed my arms again. I did not know what to say. I felt as country as country could be.

Children ran past us on the steps. They screamed excitedly for the sunshine that flowed through the high windows on the landing.

Marvin knew something I didn't. He looked me over silently and gauged my flaws. He said he would meet with Trinise and me later. He disappeared into a door that wasn't labeled. I stared after him for a moment. I wished to be as swift and efficient as him—to always know what I was about to do.

I went to the playground and stood around. I read the cuss words written on the children's toys. A young man stopped on the sidewalk when he saw me. He leaned against an oak tree. He told me, "This neighborhood gon' eat you alive." Then he moved on. I heard his laughter all the way down the block.

The next week Trinise and Marvin and I had a meeting. We ate our lunches together.

Marvin's words were despondent. He was tired of Meadows.

He knew the truth—he'd read all the books and could see the future.

Marvin told me that if I walked anywhere on the Northside I should put the hood of my sweatshirt over my blond hair so that I wouldn't attract as much attention. He told me never to wear my boots on the Northside again.

Trinise didn't say not to do anything. Trinise packed her lunch in a purple, insulated lunch bag. She ate smartly: celery sticks, yogurt, leftover soup in a plastic container, and bread wrapped in tinfoil.

I watched her during the last recess break. I studied her as she glistened with sweat. I noticed that even when her body was drained of all energy, she wore a smile and a stately, celestial graciousness. She could have been draped in a choir robe and singing angelically. She directed the actions of the antsy schoolchildren with ease. They listened to her.

Trinise was a Pisces, a projects girl, an aesthetic fashion queen. She lived in new shoes and tattoos. She wore lip gloss and high-heeled boots. She smelled of fresh, musky perfume. Her hair was neatly done. She did nails for spare money. Went to a Baptist church.

I said her name over again in my mind, *Trinise*. I listened to her speak. I tasted the sounds of her words—the way she swallowed the insides of them and made each syllable a guttural utterance.

That night my empty, black sleep was replaced by dreams of Trinise. I felt myself looking at her from across a vast sea. Saltwater and ocean currents stopped me from coming closer. On the other side of the water, Trinise's eyelashes swept across supple cheeks. She moved like graceful gelatin. I didn't know how to swim.

8

STREET WALKING

Marvin, Trinise, and I couldn't take the children outside. Hustlers used the basketball nets after school got out. There were too many shootings, too many rapes, and too many wars. Police officers were few and far between. They worked without partners. They were scared and didn't get out of their squad cars. Trinise, Marvin, and I locked the children safely inside during the after-school program. We stayed with them. We ignored our urges to go home. I thought about swimming in bright blue Lake Cushman. I imagined fishing for steelhead in the Wynoochee River. I knew the water in the Chehalis ran vivid and green. In my mind I walked and walked and never stopped dreaming.

I missed my brother like cool, fresh air. Colin and I walked everywhere. We walked uptown and down. We sat in the All Night Diner for too long. We ordered one cup of coffee between us—paid for it with nickels and quarters. We were loud and rude without knowing it. We chased away the tourist customers. Monique or Ratboy or someone else always stopped by to see us. Too many Cota kids were bad for business. We were eventually asked to leave. We stuck to side streets and alleys—our Converse tennis shoes and Doc Martens boots wore out. We tramped in wide, irregular circles. The streets of David were one rain puddle after another—murky chocolate water and potholes. It was a town everyone else drove through—and kept on going. But *we* walked. We saw what people did inside their houses. The air around the migrant worker camps was perfumed with heavy Guatemalan, Salvadorian, and Mexican cooking spices—cumin, anise, cayenne pepper, and garlic. We smelled oregano and paprika. We looked at the pots of fresh basil along the sidewalks. We imagined the food while we kicked at stones. We looked at the litter in the gutters. We examined the colorful flags in the windows of the travel trailers.

After Mother and Mima left, Colin and I had only each other. We spread ourselves out across town. We followed the Cota kids who got together. We were all tired of having nowhere to go. There were no youth centers—no facilities to keep the rain off our heads. Cota kids formed groups and rented old buildings downtown. They crammed together in trailers in the woods. Sometimes home was a dangerous place. School was an idiotic dream that faded fast. There was no taste of book-learned words in our mouths. Kids moved out on their own at young ages. They joined forces. Six or eight teenagers in three bedrooms. They played their guitars as loud as they could. They knew they couldn't go back and redo their childhood—we could never be kids again. You only get one shot. Us Cota kids were somewhere in between childhood and adult knowledge. Something ugly that nobody wanted to see or know about.

Our houses got dirty. We were sick from lack of sleep, cheap food, too much beer, and foot traffic. Things like heat and water were intermittent. We huddled around space heaters during the winter. Every dirty plate and open container was an ashtray. There were fat fleas and starving dogs. There were mice in the kitchen, pot in the bedroom, rain on the roof, and arguments over who got the last beer. Nobody stopped by to check on us.

Hopelessness peeked into every window. It sniffed at welcome mats, stuck its long fingers into the cracks in the walls. It whispered like breezes. Rusty vehicles broke down. The Cota kids started looking tired. Desperation came in on the bottom of our shoes after a hard day. It was swallowed with our beer. It was everywhere—in every board and sheet of drywall, every piece of worn carpet, every speck of dirt and defeated dream. It dripped through the leaky roofs. It hovered over unopened mail—the bills that piled up on the cinder block furniture.

Drugs crept up on our backs and took over quickly. They would not give up. They laughed and screamed in ecstasy at our attempts to free ourselves. The houses downtown became more and more unkempt. Bald spots appeared in front yards. Real estate prices stagnated and then plummeted. We watched as crystal meth became a living, breathing entity—the tourists bought more and more land—downtown became crowded. We were suddenly presented with a way to escape. City kids came to buy drugs from us. They sold them to suburban ravers. Meth was cheap to make. There was a never-ending supply. There were no seasons or dry spells or dependency on shipments. We became caught up in the death and destruction—the black eyes, swollen lips, neglected children and piles of garbage. Meth was a reason to fight with one another. Meth was a reason for more guns. There were more crimes for the television shows that glorified police officers, demonized the poor, and served everything up as some kind of entertaining answer for the people who remained unaffected. We felt guilty with a steadfast conviction—a deep shame that burned and destroyed. It would not wipe off our pale skin. We were somehow always wrong—unfit for any other occupation. We did things that children should never do. We saw things that would haunt our nights. The city of David suddenly needed more beds for the prison business. Everyone forgot why the crimes started in the first place—no other long-term alternatives were offered. Young people were stuck with questions that had no answers. We began to think we didn't deserve any. The news reporters just couldn't figure it out. They talked about us as if we were a fungus blight that had mysteriously appeared in a field of flowers. We were all intrinsically wrong. It was our own fault. The violence continued. Young girls kept conceiving life. The babies ended up struggling along with the rest of us.

I remember everything in flashes—broken dinner plates on the floor, red faces, bare feet, and stolen jewelry. Thick smoke spiraled up into the glass pipes. Music played through radios in crowded living rooms. Our eyes were wet and red-rimmed. We gave each other tattoos and piercings. We used a language that was not written down in dictionaries. Our broken toilet seats were covered in urine. We were subject to sudden, violent, and irrational acts.

Meth houses never lasted very long. They burned up in their

own fire. Kids got arrested or went somewhere else. Everything was turned over and stolen. Colin and I came back to the empty houses. We made our rounds—avoided the used needles sticking out of the carpets. There was never anything but random mouse droppings, dirty socks, or an odd pillowcase with blood on it. Nothing made any sense. None of it had any reason. The objects couldn't tell the stories we needed to hear. It all happened too fast for anything to imprint itself on the walls or the linoleum or the inanimate objects lying around a scarred woodstove. Hopeless-ness made for short attention spans. We rambled quietly through the rooms—abandoned and lonely.

Every night, Colin and I walked through the neighbor-hoods along Cota Street. We wanted to know that these houses mattered—that there was a difference between depth and domi-nance. We watched each light and intersection. We viewed every tourist restaurant and failing business. Outside of Cota Street, there was always opposition and blame. There were rich kids at the skate park in Olympia, fair-weather punk rockers outside shows at the Capitol Theater, hippie snobs who bought drugs from us, tourists who only drove through our town without stopping. I often grew angry and violent at their casual dismissal. At how things did not actually touch them. I placed myself inches from their faces and said, "I'll take you there—past the Crab Apple Apartments where the heroin grows wings, down by the railroad tracks to watch the dead men wander. I'll walk with you where *I* come from. I'll show you the houses that burned down without stopping, the condensation on the trailer windows. I'll show you the places *I've* seen. Kids like you can't get too close to the bushes. Because arms reach out across the shadows and pull you under.

You're scared you'll be just like us. You're afraid you'll become another piece of trash." So easily, I knew, it could happen to them.

Colin rolled his eyes at my big mouth. Dragged me away as I threatened. Told me none of them would understand. Explained that seeing wasn't always believing. "I told you, Vera. *We'll find our own way.*" And I tried to listen. But sometimes my anger left me shaking and bitter and kept me up at night. Sometimes, I plotted revenge. But Colin's words always returned to me eventually. At the end of each episode, I wondered what exactly he meant.

I watched the gangs of kids saunter down Sullivan Avenue on the Northside of St. Louis. They spit slang words and stared down the whole world. I saw their colors and their swaggers. They could not be argued with. They knew the truth. They were angry. They would only get angrier. I felt the tears build up behind my eyes. I sat in the homework lab and held my head. Trinise walked slowly across the room and sat down next to me. She put her strong arm across my shoulder. She squeezed. "Miss Vera, you gon' lose it?"

I shook my head no. I decided that the "at-risk youth" in the Northside were toughest in the Northside. And country kids were toughest in the country. And Cota kids were toughest on Cota Street. And rich kids were toughest in boardrooms and courtrooms and everywhere else that mattered.

Diamond pulled on my sweatshirt—rubbed at a spot on my boot. "Miss Vera, you know what I'm gunna do when I'm grown?"

She spoke so saucily I couldn't help but ask, "What?"

"Live in the *woods.*" She set her head and her lips at her last word. She dared anyone to disagree. Her neck was steel. She looked at me with dignity—grown-up to grown-up.

"Oh! Oh! Me, too, Miss Vera!" Diandre agreed valiantly. The excited whispers flamed up and down the benches in the homework lab.

The children's eyes shone, *Live in the woods!* The words were repeated like a motto that kept them afloat.

I thought about Colin walking downtown with the grimy water from the streets soaking up his pant legs—his ghost-eyes dreaming—his heart still searching. Puddles of mud threatened. The fog hovered overhead. I thought of Monique—her face smooth with youth—her eyebrows glaring above clenched, cold teeth. She wore her makeup. She fooled her college instructors. She didn't let on that she knew things they didn't. Colin walked by crazy places alone. His heart felt stunted. Dad pulled double shifts and waited for Mother to come back. Colin put on his hand-me-down clothing and worked fast-food jobs. He wore the soles of his shoes down to slippery, bald-rubber flaps.

I had to remind myself that I couldn't go back to David. The lights would flash behind me there. I'd be asked the same questions with my tired face lit up in my rearview mirror. There would forever be the red-and-blue bursts and the search beam in my eyes. There would always be the interrogation about Brady and Colin and Jimmy James. My name was on a list. Each officer wanted to be the hero who conquered the evil villains—the sad teenagers who felt empty inside.

I wished for a moment that I could be one of the reporters on the news shows Colin and I listened to so long ago. I craved to view life with detachment as if it were one long series of events that happened in a vacuum and were beyond my control. Things unraveled into various piles—violence was pigeonholed, street gangs were named. Then we all died or went to prison. I wanted to drive a big car with tinted windows. It would have heat and air conditioning. I could pick and choose where I drove—which places I passed through and which I avoided altogether.

But then the moment was gone, and my ancestry burned and boiled. My blood grew angry. I would *walk* those streets—every one.

I looked at Diamond and nodded my approval. "I'll live in the woods, too," I told her. The homework lab was silent. I told those who listened about blue Lake Cushman and vivid green river water. I told them, "Isn't it nice to think, that if you just keep walking on street after street in the right direction, eventually you'll get there? Eventually, you'll be walking in the woods."

9

SOUL FOOD

It was time to slaughter the young roosters at Granny's house. They had to be killed before their meat became tough and hard to chew. I wasn't there to help. But I knew when Dad chopped off their heads with an axe and hung them from a cable to let the blood drain. I knew what it felt like when Colin plunged the birds into a big metal tub filled with water that was scalding over a fire. And the sound of ripping feathers from skin. The smell of fresh chicken guts and soggy carcasses. The flow of the water from the barn pump. I knew the hands of my brother and my father were covered in blood up to their elbows. They froze the birds to eat all winter and chopped firewood for themselves and Granny. Granny picked apples. She peeled and sliced them to freeze or dehydrate. She cut the ends off the soft fruit to use for applesauce. Her kitchen was a wall of cigarette smoke, cinnamon, and sugar.

The weather turned from hot to cold all at once in Missouri. There was no fall. Just summer. Then winter.

Marvin took Trinise and me out for dinner on my birthday. The restaurant was hidden down a side street. It didn't look like a business from the outside. There were no signs or specials. Only the robust smell of good food and loud music. Trinise gave me a hand-knitted purple scarf wrapped in white tissue paper. She ate her dinner carefully—said "please" and "thank you"—put her leftovers in Tupperware she brought from home—left a ten-dollar bill for the waitress who was her cousin. She left to meet her boyfriend for a movie.

Marvin didn't feel like leaving so soon. He brought two bottles of beer from the bar. He was curious—wanted to know all the answers to his questions. "So, Ms. Vera," he began. "Why did you come to St. Louis?"

I tentatively flailed to explain. It came out wrong. I promised him he didn't understand. His long torso leaned forward. His brows furrowed heatedly. He sensed the impending larger picture—the foreboding web of confusion. Perhaps, he sensed, there were more books to read. He let the subject drop. He looked me in the eye. All the different angles melded into one. We both sensed the color of life and death. Marvin knew my army was bigger, and less unified, and much harder to convince.

"David, Washington," he said with wonder as he fingered his goatee. The place of my birth was now elevated in his interest. His mind was dark and logical. There was a spark encased in it that nothing could smother. He was a fighter of a different kind. A thoughtful, deliberate one. My flailing fists suddenly seemed messy and primitive. I should have listened to Colin more often.

Marvin leaned back in the dark booth. I moved my black-eyed peas around on my plate—tilted my beer bottle up. It was a quiet moment. I let him think.

He was deft and calm as he threw the waitress's large tip on the table. There was a look of finality in his eyes. The beer warmed up my insides. I added to the money pile. Trinise's cousin would let us sit there as long as we liked. The restaurant was not busy. Neither of us moved.

Marvin stared at me critically when I blurted out, "I'm not good at explaining."

I shut up and my mind wandered. I thought of the things Jimmy James said in a low voice with his head next to mine in the dark. I heard them like a sad song. His words were not sounds. They were instincts pressed against my brain. There were things I wanted to tell Marvin. Things I thought he should know. Revelations about happiness and violence.

Behind me stood my late nights of digging into books and papers—using the library at the state college that didn't belong to me. Above my head hovered the deep feelings of despondency. I wondered if maybe the news reporters were right. Maybe the devil *was* on Cota Street. I had only imagined the great ocean and the Plan. I'd been driven crazy by youth, and hormones, and desperation. In the city of St. Louis I was a country kid. And country kids are wrong a lot.

But when I closed my eyes I remembered the cold, dark place Jimmy James was in. And staring at the bloodstains of the man from Angel Road. And Brady Robbins holding on to me when both of us felt lost. How his touch was numb and listless. And he kept saying, "Annie's dead."

My face melted in the soul food restaurant. Timothy was fed and asleep without me. I thought about all the books that told lies. But how you couldn't just burn books for lying. I started to talk to Marvin about the rules that kept us apart. I didn't know how to say parts of it. The Man from Angel Road was locked up as I trembled and did not speak. I wondered how much he would change. I knew the pressures inside would be great. Prison does that. Everyone comes out different than when they went in.

Marvin stared at me. His skin was the color of crude oil—shimmery and dark. It was navy with fine points of white. His heart was big. He brimmed with history. He went to his neighborhood meetings and lived in his sneer. He wore one gold ring on his left hand. He had long, flat-muscled arms. He sat serenely but his eyes stormed—glaring white orbs surrounded brown irises. His black hole pupils were as angry as my lover's.

I didn't answer his look. I couldn't. I took the last swallow of my beer. My army was the biggest, and the most confused, and the most easily led astray. It was hard to trust—it was hard for all of us.

I watched the candle flame dance in the glass holder on our table. I wondered about the streets that separated the Northside from the rich neighborhoods. The boundaries of the rez. The cement stockade of a prison. Bumper stickers that read FREE PALESTINE. I knew La Llorona would haunt the blockade planned for the banks of the Rio Grande. My heart made frantic objections to it all. Everything closed in.

But I remembered good things like church ladies cooking meals for homeless folks, and parks with playgrounds. I remembered music and art and writing. And the feeling of when there are no more words left.

Suddenly, Marvin handed me my birthday present—a book of poems he printed himself. I read the first page:

> my eyes must see you, woman
> your clothes and your body
> I miss the feel of you in a room
> the way you change things
> it's a hard place where they sent you
> loud and cold in the winter
> and your letters still remind me
> of all you haven't done

Colin's chicken blood–covered hands finally rested back in David. He sat on the back porch and wondered where I was.

There were two old men at the bar playing checkers in St. Louis. Marvin didn't say anything for a long time. He puffed on his cigar and waited.

"My man's locked up," I said abruptly. I hadn't known the words were going to come out of my mouth. I didn't know why they were there. The pressure had gotten to me. I felt suddenly exposed. My head spun. Marvin nodded politely. He sighed—long and hard. He stared straight ahead—kept thinking his private thoughts.

"So's my wife," he finally relented, "Patrice." I felt a lot of pain there—hurt inside his belly. He was twenty-four and very tired. His words came out of a lonely pit. He looked at me and his eyes were unguarded. It was the first time I'd ever seen him.

"Do you think she'll be different when she gets out?" I whispered.

He stared at me when he answered, "I really do not know."

Marvin drove me back to my apartment. He shut off his engine, told me he'd walk with me up the steps. He opened his door, swung one long leg out toward the street. He touched the pavement—the toe of his boot scraped the snow and gravel. I tried to scream but I couldn't find any words. So I made the noise behind the words. The sounds caught in my throat. I clutched and grabbed at his right arm, pulled his body down toward me. He turned questioningly—raised his eyebrows in alarm. The heavy door of his Crown Vic slammed shut.

He'd been moving quickly. Our heads were swirling. The beer had gone to his head.

It was a tired and dirty city bus that had come for him. The headlights soon filled the car. The horn blared. It filled our night with a terrible shock. Weary figures stood inside. They held on to the rails. They were pressed closely against each other. Their eyes were glazed over from working long hours at minimum wage. The bus took them quickly out of the rich neighborhoods and back to their respective projects. They stared out the windows. Recounted in their heads each and every deflation they had encountered that day. The seconds after the bus passed were long—the space of time couldn't be measured in ordinary ways. Marvin and I were left in a mist. The 99 was going too fast to stop. The bus was wide and morbid. More seconds ticked by in which neither of us said anything. Wet garbage crawled across the road in the icy wind.

"I like your poems!" I finally spluttered. "A lot."

Marvin looked desolate. He was suddenly shaky and

sweating. Nothing really mattered as much as the woman behind cement walls. He had almost missed seeing her again. He mumbled something about me owning his soul now and adjusted his glasses with the deliberate patience that defined him.

He walked me to my door. I felt for the deadbolt and slid my key in. Marvin waited until I got inside and locked all four locks. He turned and walked down the two flights of steps back to his car. He drove the city streets for a while just to think. He made his way over the bridge to Illinois. His mind returned to his perpetual organization directed toward one goal. His thoughts pecked at the strategy unmercifully. He expanded and narrowed and grew more and more dangerous. In the dark, he made plans to liberate East St. Louis.

10

CHRISTMAS

I tried to stay inside my apartment on Christmas. Everything seemed so impossible—so out of control. I stayed in bed. I jumped at small noises. I dreamed. I wanted to believe that St. Louis was an elaborate play—an inaccurate, too-crazy script. I was cold and sleepy and saw everything through a haze. None of it was real. I wanted to wake up and be safe in my old bed. Any minute he would come back: *the Man from Angel Road.* I couldn't stop pacing. I wandered in my empty apartment like a ghost. My feet drug me across the hardwood floors with my brain tumbling and maniacal behind them. I was bedridden and sleepless. I was moody and flatlined. My world was tumultuous and gray.

I lit candles and sticks of incense. I took a bubble bath with vanilla extract sprinkled into the steaming water. I rubbed lotion onto my skin. I sipped broth from a cup. I boiled water for tea but didn't feel like drinking city water steeped in bitter, store-bought herbs.

I changed my sheets. I lay on my back on my camping mat in my apartment. I closed my eyes and let my mind wander. I flew away over the miles and miles of farmland and sundown towns and lost highways on fire. It was easy—like stepping into another room. Christmas, alone I remembered:

The medicinal herbs hang in bunches in the kitchen. I have picked them from land I know well. They offer me their faint plant smells. I stare at Jimmy James's message written on the yellow paper. I pull the herb bunches down and unwrap the netting. I sit on the fire escape and burn them in the barbecue grill. I smell the chamomile, lavender, rose hips, and dried raspberry leaves catch fire one after the other. The yarrow comes last.

The silence and fog are intense. The rain—the wet, dark rain looms like a foreboding giant. Winter is here. It is something I cannot conquer alone. The evergreen trees hunch over me. I hold Timothy tight. The impending rainy season wants to eat us whole. We haven't saved up enough food for the cold months. Weeds creep into the vacant lots. The steelhead bleed out of their skin in the Columbia. It is dark and wet like a demon womb. The rent is late. Timothy won't stop crying. I pack his bags and call Nadine. I hang up the phone and stare out the window like Mother used to.

Jimmy James stands behind a thick, tall curtain of mystery. I can't imagine him. I can't remember the way he smells or the low tone of his voice. I don't remember why he's gone. It is all such a shock. He is not asleep in our bed. He is in a cold, dark place that can't be reached by dreams or letters. There are cement walls.

His wounds ache. We are young and uneducated—young and uneducated people are wrong a lot. The voice on the phone keeps telling me, "There is no bail."

I got dressed and went out to my truck, which was covered in snow. I was angry and wanted to punch the cold metal. Even though it didn't make any sense. Even though it would not help anything. The vinyl seat felt frigid on the back of my legs even though I was wearing long johns and thick wool pants. I put the heater on full blast and let the motor warm up.

I drove the empty city streets and looked for him angrily— the Man from Angel Road. I searched and searched the streets of Midtown that were like ghost ships—the business sectors that were empty. All the men in suits had long ago gone home to the suburbs. I drove to places I thought he might be: *the central west end—the bridge with gaslights.* The taxi drivers didn't look at me—a sad spirit in a slow truck.

Jimmy James had to come back. I'd left his Kerouac books on a shelf at Dad's house. I saved Lou Reed. I saved all his records for when we could listen together. I remembered how he propped his boots up on our wooden chairs.

He loved me even when I didn't know how to act—loved me even more for my lack of manners and unrepentant grin. He held me after my impotent anger left me shaking and void. He reminded me that the price we paid in misery and frustration was small in comparison. I asked him why the world wasn't fair. I asked him why some had so much and the rest so little. I asked what price *they* had to pay to never have to struggle—to be so untouchable and cruel and judgmental. He laughed and answered, "Baby, you already *know.* They don't have *souls.*" And finally,

I laughed with him. Laughed at myself. Kissed his cheek and put my head where it fit best—on his chest that felt like knotty pinewood.

I knew Jimmy James would come back. He would be immaculate like new snow on cold granite. I would breathe in the scent of sweat on his neck and taste his salty lips when he got off work. We would go on long camping trips—show Timothy Lake Ozette and the Hoh Rain Forest. I would have my family back. I would care for their male bodies—draw warm baths and wash away every memory of jail cells and being apart.

But the air in my truck was thick with the memory of clotted blood. My vision swam with it. The coagulated liquid choked me. It was syrupy and dark. I flailed against it in a mounting, frustrated terror.

I had to turn around empty-handed. I was forced back into my neighborhood alone. I stumbled across the parking lot at the corner market near my apartment. My fingers were cold as I lifted the pay phone receiver. I took a deep breath and called Trinise.

11

ON RESERVATION ROAD

The project Trinise lived in was crowded and bright. She introduced me to her mama, stepfather, and too many aunts, uncles, and cousins to remember. I came in time to say grace. I ate everything that was offered to me. I sat in a kitchen chair and drank warm liquor while I laughed at every joke. I helped with the dishes. I talked about the weather with Trinise's waitress cousin—how quickly it had changed from hot to cold and how unused to such changes I was. I washed. She dried. Someone else put the dishes away.

Afterward, I made my way slowly through the living room making small talk with various relatives. I watched Trinise's mama scold a very old man in a black sweater who tried to smoke vanilla-flavored tobacco out of a pipe inside her apartment. Her body stood incensed inside her green chiffon dress. Her neck was firm. I recognized Trinise's poise.

I looked at the man and shrugged. He was being shooed out the back door. I asked if I could join him, and he told me grandly that it would be his pleasure.

Outside, the cold wind hit me like a wave of ice water. I stared in awe at the rectangle of brick buildings that surrounded us. There was a chain-link fence with razor wire. The St. Louis sky poured down snow. The charred brick of the city had turned to blood-red ice topped with soft, sooty white. I smoked with the old man. Our exhalations were thick and white from smoke and frozen breath. We appreciated the quiet. I remembered how two years ago today, Monique left David.

I said good-bye to Trinise early to avoid the snow. I knew her neighborhood would not be plowed. I thought about Monique. I drove through the bright white afternoon of the midwestern winter with her confusion chasing me. Two years ago, Monique left. She deserted Cota Street as if it were on fire and about to consume her. She renounced our hometown when the sky began its long descent into months of incessant cold rain and oppressive darkness. She went to a place that was colder and drier. I wondered about her. Somewhere in Montana she was feeling the chills like I was—feeling the winter how only lonely women can. She drove over the mountain passes the last day that she could—before they got snowed over for the winter. She packed her truck with boxes of brushes, paint, and canvases. She took emergency supplies of water, wool blankets, food rations, and flares.

The summer months had been hard on Monique that year. Her eyes had grown faded and worn as my brother's frenzied fearlessness developed. His obstinacy was frightening. Monique tried to be strong. She drove her rusted Chevy LUV like everything was fine. Colin warned her not to wander too far alone. Monique wore strapless, hand-sewn dresses and made candles and beaded necklaces to sell at the farmers' market. Colin made threats and stayed up late into the night sitting on the Cota Street couch with the overhead lights off. He checked three times before opening the front door. Monique took pictures of the I.W.A. seal painted on the brick of the old union hall. Her snake tattoo crawled up her neck. She tried to talk Colin out of everything. But he wouldn't listen. He kept his gun loaded. His finger on the trigger.

She told me every detail before she left. I listened like a stone to every word. There was frost on the haunted fir trees. I watched them to avoid looking at her face. I tried hard to understand. She tried even harder to explain. She talked and then held her breath. Her posture held a deep sense of shame. It hurt to watch. The engine was running in her truck. She was parked in front of the All Night Diner. The exhaust made a white cloud behind the vehicle. I reminded her to check her oil. I glanced at her face. Her voice was gravelly Patsy Cline. I encouraged her to go on. She told me about the trailer park in Montana—the one she was going to live in with her aunt. She talked desperately about the dense thicket of resin birch, children playing in grassy patches, a larch-pole fence and the dusty trail that followed it. She tried to explain the tentative, miraculous feeling that rose up in her belly. She stopped talking and held that belly. She turned to her truck and put her forehead on her arm. She left a smudge of makeup below her elbow. She told the rest of the story with her back to me—her eyes scrunched into the curve of her flesh—her voice gone wavery.

She said it was horrible finding him. Her tightly wound body sprung in an instant. She felt that she was breaking—finally losing it. The pool of blood that fanned out from his head had begun to congeal on the linoleum. It turned dark on the outer edges. She thought he was dead.

It was strange sitting in the hospital room after Colin woke up. Emotions beyond description had passed through her body during the time he was asleep. She squeezed his hand all through the afternoon. He threw up thin vomit laced with blood clots. She hadn't slept in days. Her feelings grew distant. They turned into cold shards of glass on the horizon. Her hot lungs stopped moving. Her thumping heartbeat quieted. The intern who was on watch calculated her every move. Colin had been red-flagged for emotional instability. The intern looked young and nervous and flippant. He must have been from somewhere far away that had medical schools and no methamphetamines. He read his book and pretended to be bored. Monique knew he was listening to every word she uttered. Possibly taking notes. He was watching her flush Colin's black-red vomit down the toilet. He was wondering about the white trash teenager he was in charge of—speculating about what it took for people to reach rock bottom, to stop grasping after strings.

Tears were locked inside Monique's heart—they thumped against her glass rib cage. They spread rumors through her body. For the first time in her life she was delicate—a thin vase that was leaking—her insides dripping from her cracks. Her feelings came to her sporadically along with a remorse that floundered.

She left Colin in the hospital room alone to smoke a rolled cigarette on a rain-drenched wooden bench in front of the waiting room. She glared into the sky. Her world was frustrating and ugly and going nowhere. A nurse who knew her mother saw Monique's shaking shoulders and reached out to her. She held her firmly—with a brisk hand. The nurse told her she needed to be strong. Monique's heart raced and then stopped moving—it turned to water. It washed away the confusing noise and the bloody vomit. She told the nurse she had failed at love, and she was sorry.

Her thoughts raced when she went back to the hospital room. They swirled in the stormy, dreary silence while Colin slept in fits and woke anxiously. The dark came and hid her face.

Visiting hours were almost over.

Monique was water. Her drips found every crevice on the hospital floor. They made the white tiles wet. Her heart screamed inside her chest. It was a long, lonely sound like the train whistle leaving town. But she talked to Colin during his brief wakefulness. She told him she wanted to go swimming at the Ledges as soon as he got out. She tried to be cheerful. She talked about camping at Lake Cushman. She said, "Vera and Jimmy James will come." He didn't answer and she started trembling. She tried to remember: *None of it had been her idea.*

Colin wanted her to go to school. "The Art Institute of Seattle," he told Dad proudly. He saw her poring wistfully over the pamphlets—wanting something she could never have. He convinced her they could save up money and move away. "Right now, we're living paycheck to paycheck," Colin explained. He urged her, "We're never gonna get out of here any other way." She knew he was right. There was no denying their unfinished GEDs and fast-food wages. Their total lack of contacts.

It was easy to start selling meth. The hard part was staying up all night in fear—imagining old friends breaking in on them. Colin lived in paranoid agony with a loaded .40-caliber handgun under his pillow. He didn't sleep if Monique slept. He didn't eat if she needed more. All for Monique. All so Monique could go to school.

Colin spoke before she had to leave the hospital. "Are you still here?" His voice searched for her weakly. Her attention rested on every twitch of his eyelids, every uncomfortable, restless movement he made. Her name caught inside his throat. Her water washed over him in slow splashes. It broke down his flesh. It carried his voice away and decomposed him.

"I know you got a plan," he told her when she found his hand. "I know you got things you gotta do." A green light on one of the machines he was hooked up to blinked. "Why are you wasting so much time hanging around this old town?"

The lights buzzed in fits. The terror of her life alone spun out in front of her. It shot off splashes of tears, and unpaid bills, and acceptance letters she did not reply to. She wanted to lock away her dreams in a metal box. She wanted Colin to be with her and forget everything else. But it was too late for that.

"We ain't *doing* nothing," he reminded her.

She let the truth hang in the air—unchallenged and stupid. Thousands of nights of "nothing" stretched before her. The loneliness stared into her eyes relentlessly. All the things they had done haunted. Her future without Colin scathed the walls. The fear of her meaningless death was now possible. It reached for her. It was hard to get away from. None of us Cota kids would be remembered in history books. The tidewater mill was silent. The polluted harbor was lifeless. There was no past. The future was covered by a thick blanket of fog.

"You need to paint all those pretty things you see." Colin

raised his bandaged head. The movement made him dizzy. He couldn't see her. Everything was a living, dark red color—the inside of his eyelids and the murkiness that blurred his vision. His gums were rimmed in blood. He tried to keep his mouth shut while he talked. He didn't want to scare her. "You gotta put down on paper all those pictures in your head." He was exasperated and stubborn. He knew that every second on Cota Street was less vivid for Monique. "You gotta do all those things you was gonna do! If you don't, all of this is for nothing!"

She knew he was right. There was no choice now. She thought of her plans—her paintbrushes resting in mason jars of cloudy water, her cloth and cleaner and canvases. *Her plans* had once seemed so beautiful and colorful. But now each time she closed her eyes she pictured Colin's blood drying on the linoleum in the kitchen. His jammed Glock in the corner. The red-splattered baseball bat thrown down chaotically. The smeared bloody hand-prints on the wall at Colin's head. Her own paintbrushes scattered wildly over the carpet. One in particular near Colin had black bristles that had been dipped in red. A good painter *never* left her brushes out with paint on them. And she was a good painter. That paintbrush troubled her. There was only one color—the color of life and death.

Colin had forgotten about the window in the crawl space he kicked out himself when he was young. The hole was stopped up with a towel. A towel was easy to kick in silently. As Colin checked the door for the third time the five figures came up behind him. He was almost relieved as the darkness fell in red and black and screaming dizziness. The moment had finally come. He felt the first blow sharply. The rest were faded and deadened.

A voice was talking in a low frequency at his ear. It spoke in a thick, rural accent. "Tell yer sister . . ." He strained to identify the sound. He grappled with his burst and rotating brain. Was it just the drugs and money they had come for? One eye looked through a mask of torn skin at a pair of combat boots. They were black and bloody. Behind them a head bent busily with one of Monique's paintbrushes dipped in his own blood. A head hovered near him. "Tell yer sister," the voice had said. He didn't know if the sound was coming from the boy or if the boy was gone and he was hearing only a memory. The voice was saying, *Tell yer sister she's on the wrong side a' things. Tell her boyfriend move over. And he can take that bastard baby right on outta town.*

They left soon after. And before anyone else could come Colin slid on his belly toward the wall and Monique's discarded paintbrush. His head swam and he could not see for a moment. In a dream, he reached toward the wall and smeared the words Duane had written in blood, the words that would tear Monique apart if she saw: *RACE TRAITOR.* With that done, he turned over, closed his eyes, and awaited death.

Monique squeezed Colin's hand until her knuckles cracked. She seeped into him—straight to his weakly thumping heart. Would never tell him that despite his best efforts she had a feeling about why the boys had come. Her tears explained what she couldn't say because of everything: *Your biggest mistake was loving me.* The intern openly glared at them.

Colin let forever lapse. And then he shunned her. "Go on now." He let go of her hand and turned to the wall. His hospital gown separated at his back. "Get out there." She saw the acne that scabbed up his bony shoulder blades. His pale skin hid nothing but thin bones. It had been a long time since he was tan and muscular. It had been years since they'd swam in the cool pools of Goldsborough Creek in summer. How could everything fall apart so fast?

His sacrifices came rushing at her all at once. She felt them tugging at her conscience inexorably and then flowing past her. She could have shrieked and cried wildly. She did not want to leave him. She refused to be caught adrift in the storm of violence. She wanted, rather, to be part of that rush—the tempest that had led him to the hospital room in a changed town.

She poured her body over his. She wanted to heal him—spill her heart into his sheets and bones. He didn't respond, just like a dead person. It was too late.

The intern told her she needed to leave—that she was making a bad situation worse. She turned on the stranger aggressively. Her body was a raging river. "You don't understand anything! You never *had* to!" Her words were a storm. She was escorted out with firm fingers clamped on her upper arm. The intern's hand looked ugly and hairy and pale against her skin. He had been waiting to do something righteously violent. His touch left a bruise. She squirmed in his arms and hated him. She wanted to believe that it was he who was taking her away and not everything else. She didn't see Colin's face for the last time. He wouldn't turn to her.

She drove to the river on the reservation. It was angry and bitter and wise in the wintertime. She smoked cheap cigarettes. She tried to calm down. She tried to think about how the tourists fished for king salmon because king salmon were big and easy to catch. They took pictures and didn't eat them. The fishermen stood in crowds on the banks and tangled in each other's line.

They didn't understand why nobody built big motels for them to stay in. They pulled their heaving, fat, dark catches up onto the rocks, and the fish gasped among the pieces of fishing line, discarded bait, candy bar wrappers, and beer cans. Young boys from the rez watched curiously on the other side of the river across the bank. They were silent as the tourists held the large fish by the gills and the other tourists took pictures and congratulated them. They didn't care what the spawning salmon tasted like. They didn't care how poor or small the rez was. They didn't go downtown to Cota Street or shop at La Tienda Latino. The tourists left the salmon in their coolers. They put them into their freezers. They ate steak for dinner.

Monique walked to the mouth of the river—where the freshwater met the saltwater of the canal. There were little grass islands, tide flats, and salt-loving plants. She walked in the new-winter chill. The moon reflected on the underside of the quaking aspens. She watched the stars that were like snow swirling, the clouds chased away. There was a clear black sky and bright white lights. She stood on the edge of the lapping river. The wind rose up off the seawater. She closed her eyes, felt the light of the full moon, and made up her own religion. She called to her spirits for guidance. She didn't wait for them to answer. Monique wanted to dive into the water after she had swallowed the sleeping pills in her pocket. She wanted to swim in the cold water until she slept. Her life was payment for all the harm done. All the children at the meth houses with dirty faces. The barking, beaten, starving dogs. The smell of burnt plastic and cat piss. The tattoos on the kids who beat Colin. The baseball bat that cracked his skull. The river whispered. Her body answered. The dark current wanted her. Her death would make the world stop—the machine would sputter. It would all grow black and distant as the water found her and the tide brought her out to Hood Canal.

The salty grass waved. The starlight reached the bottom of still pools. The backwater in the slow-moving parts lapped sullenly. The dandelion faces were squeezed shut as they waited for the sun. She imagined the earth consuming and comforting her. She wanted to sink low beneath the ground—to sing sad praises to the dirt, and the leaves and the salmonberries rotting there. She imagined something deeper than sleep—something bottomless and cavernous with spaces so wide and dark they lost her dishonor. She wanted to turn her skin inside out. She wanted to scream and be forgiven. But her voice wasn't sound. It was only fading vibrations.

The current kept sliding by. The salmon, on the edge of death, sensed her pain. They would allow her to sit on the river bottom with them as they spawned and died. The last of their energy expired. Monique wanted her soul to wander in and out of the algae and mud and carcasses all the way to the Pacific Ocean. She wanted to feel the waves grow salty and colder. She wanted the deep water to pardon her—scatter her—make her nothing but wet.

She would take it all away in the flash flood of her death. She would slide through the moonlight with the sadness of the whole town following her. She would be the wet dirt around the bones in the unmarked graves in the mountains. The spirits of the mangled men would be released. Her raindrops would dive deep into the black mulch—the richest soil. It would hug the worms and shiny beetles. Her whispers would flutter and then become silence itself. Moonlight would lap with the movement of the freshwater and the sea.

And then, as she slowly and quietly reached this place, Jimmy James Blood called to her from a large red alder tree that was leaning out over the water. "He was just sitting there," she told me in that parking lot. "Right above me on a branch. Smoking a cigarette I hadn't smelled before. I swear he just appeared. I didn't hear him crawl up there."

"Go on home," he told her. And Monique hadn't moved—just stared up at him in shock. He kept talking firmly and gently. "You have a baby inside of you, Monique. Just go on home."

Dry land reached out to greet her. It muddied her thoughts and intentions. Even the salmon were flopping toward the shore. The drought made her bewildered. Reality was suddenly upon her. Jimmy James did not reach out strong, comforting arms. He did not whisper soft words into her ear. His black Carhartt jacket looked silver in the light from the moon. It was worn and faded and soft. He slid off the tree branch. Spit on the ground. Left her standing by herself with her mouth wide open. He turned around and said, "It's high time you git on outta David. I heard Montana's real pretty." He smiled that smile. Climbed up the bank to the road where she saw headlights shine on her own car—the deep rumbling of an engine—a vehicle filled with shady figures that were a mystery to her. Then he was gone, and she was alone.

Monique drove home and thought about traveling east on I-90 to the trailer park. Her aunt would welcome her with open arms.

"I'm going to Rocky Mountain College," she told me in the

parking lot of the All Night Diner and described a liberal arts school in a cold, dry place. Colin always put every cent into her account. There hadn't been any cash in the house on Cota Street. He knew what was coming. It was fourteen hours to Billings. But all she really wanted to do was disappear into water flowing over gravel.

"Vera, I don't wanna be an artist no more!" She finally broke down in front of the restaurant as she hid her eyes. "What a stupid idea!" Her hair escaped from several barrettes as she pounded the rusty steel of her truck with her fist. "It's not worth it!" Monique finally raised her brown eyes to me. They were bloodshot and cold and hazardously dry of tears. "Nobody's an *artist* around here!" She flung her hands out in despair. We both noticed the cracked streets and the sad faces on all the buildings as if for the first time. The sight of her and those buildings broke my cold heart.

I couldn't be mad at her. Deep inside, I knew she wouldn't have been able to stop my brother any more than I could have. We all knew what was going to happen. I couldn't blame her. The problem was not Monique. The problem was misty and still eluded me. I couldn't quite grasp on to all the reasons. But it had something to do with those cracked streets and empty buildings. And if I didn't stand next to Monique, I would be standing somewhere else. The thought crossed my mind that I should be on the seat next to her. But as much as I hated it, those cracked streets and empty buildings were all I knew. And I couldn't let go for the life of me. I didn't hold Monique or tell her everything would be all right. All I could offer her was a forced smile and the promise of a phone call when I got paid next.

She got into her truck and slammed the door. I hoped the

vehicle would make it. I saw her cursing and banging her steering wheel as she turned left to merge onto 101.

Shit.

It just wasn't fair.

Colin was released from the hospital and taken straight to jail. They let him out after his hearing where he pled *not guilty*. He went back to the house on Cota Street where he and Dad now lived alone. Monique's poster of the Specials stayed on the wall of the bedroom that was once Mima's.

Jimmy James was right. There was a new heart beating—a new pulse at Monique's core.

The baby was a boy. She said he would have her hair, Colin's black Irish blue eyes, and her mother's nose. "But he'll be stronger than we are," she assured me. "I'm going to name him Colin James O'Neel."

She said when Colin's court stuff was all over he could come stay with her. They had a no-contact order but it wouldn't last forever. She said her aunt wouldn't mind them all three staying in the room in the trailer in the trailer park—the injured boy and the anxious girl and the sweet, innocent baby. She said his name would still be on the birth certificate.

Monique told me she knew things would only get better. I tried to believe her. But a nagging feeling told me otherwise.

12

6:30 A.M.

The sounds through the walls of my apartment were muted and sleepy in the winter morning. The water ran at 6:30 a.m. Children argued loudly and a stern, adult voice chastised them into silence. Condensation covered the mirrors in my bathroom. I heard stomping feet and singing. I thought about how we all removed our clothes and showered almost in unison. I cooked whole-grain hot cereal with raisins. The steam rose up from my saucepan. I spooned lumps of cereal into a wooden bowl and drizzled honey over the top. I poured whole cream into all the dips and crevices before returning to my still-warm covers to eat slowly in the cold, dark morning.

Outside, the air was frigid. The wind whistled and moaned around the twin brick buildings. A stale, glaring sun peeked out from between them. Ivanhoe and Shenendoah stood sentry against gray-and-white skies. Ivanhoe's turrets and large windows facing the street urged me to remember better times—when her rooms housed well-to-do young couples as the city's economy boomed. Shenendoah said nothing—she was being renovated. Piles of construction refuse littered the rear near the basement entrance. Asbestos and lead paint particles glistened on the wind. Shenendoah's back wall was torn off. Families still lived inside the apartments. The new owner took out their toilets and set them on the front lawn. I watched them trying to eat breakfast in their winter parkas. A man sat in his car with the engine running. Dark circles crept underneath his eyes. I tried to wave good morning to him. He did not have the strength to see me. There were hard lines of determination on his face. He lifted a finger tiredly. The motion seemed to leave him exhausted.

Our neighborhood was getting too close to the rich neighborhoods. We would all be pushed out for the profit of real estate companies. Ivanhoe's and Shenendoah's strong and unadorned redbrick faces had to compete with the renovated, painted ladies that lined the streets east of us near Soulard.

The winter was bitter. My skin cracked from the cold. My truck was girdled with snow. The slush lay dirty and brown on the streets. It was speckled with trash and pebbles. Cars lined up behind the snow shovels on Vandeventer and Lafayette. City buses were black from the grit of sand and de-icer on the streets. The gas company raised their rates. Senior citizens on fixed incomes had trouble paying. Homeless people froze to death. The news stories made me think about lepers during biblical times—how they couldn't feel the rats nibbling on their appendages. They couldn't tell when their skin froze to the ground. Their bodies fell from them in little pieces before they died.

I rode the bus to work. I watched for Bottle Cap Man, Mirabella, and Patti Smith. I did not want them to freeze to the ground. I wanted them to hold on—to stay alive just like me. They were hope against all odds. I watched them bury their faces in the hoods of their sweatshirts and behind liquor bottles. I watched them push shopping carts filled with clutter that didn't make sense to anyone else. They smoked cigarettes to concentrate. They held their heads in their hands. Bottle Cap Man yelled loudly. He got skinnier and skinnier.

At Meadows, I waited for the children to file in from the cold. They shed their worn, heavy coats. They laughed and played and asked me about the art projects I had planned. Their faces were pliable and new. They made my heart ache. I didn't think about anything else. I didn't want to.

13

LA LLORONA

The memories trickled back slowly over the icy winter—the coldest out of any I had ever known. The numbness surrounded me. But my daydreams became frantic. They picked up speed and accuracy. Their sharpened points dug into me. They drew fresh blood from wounds that refused to heal.

Annie's brother shot a man. He robbed him and left him for dead. I watched the rain splatter and drip off his brown Carhartt jacket as he leaned close and explained nervously, "I got scared." Stiv was twenty years old. His hands shook. He chain-smoked full-flavor Marlboros and didn't look so rough-and-tumble anymore. It was only a matter of time before he was locked away. We knew he didn't have a place to run to.

"He was yellin' real loud after the bullet went in," he told us. "He was bleedin' 'n' screamin' like a skeered piglet." Annie talked lowly to him. I squeezed my eyes shut. Their words floated away from me. I heard Stiv yelp, "*Shit,* Annie! *Oh shit.* I'm goin' to prison!" He held his head. Paced. Kicked at the tires on his truck. He was coming down from the PCP. I thought of their dead mother and their father with a shotgun. How the walls of a trailer can close in on little kids. Floors can sound hollow. I saw their home with no foundation—soaked in unforgiving rain—rotting in overgrown weeds and car parts. It was a long, long way from anywhere—a forty-five-minute drive into the hills. Nobody could hear them screaming. There were no friendly open doors with yellow light. Stiv blamed himself for Annie's baby. It tore him apart. He shouldn't have left her there all alone. He looked at Annie with real fear in his eyes. "I told 'em, Annie. I told 'em I wouldn't run with 'em no more." The words chilled me to my depths. "Duane and Kat and them. I was fucking her, Annie! I was fucking Kat."

Then. Before I could even think. Before Annie could stop me I was diving at Stiv's legs.

His body was toppling with a surprised *humph.* I had him down in the cold muddy water. Sloshing in the puddles. He was grappling with my small mean fists. I was sitting over him. Just for one moment. Trying to find his face in the dark. Pummeling his neck with furious, futile blows. I did not shout. Every breath went toward the driving whirlwind of black anger. Before Stiv got a hold of himself. Before he pushed me off him. His boot driving into the side of my head was the first thing I had really felt in a long time. I felt his weight over me. He was strong. Much stronger than me. He could have walked away then. Instead he pushed my face into a puddle of oily runoff. My cheek burned in the cold water. He pinned my arms behind me. Gritty sand coated my face. He leaned down close. Under the stars in a rainy mill town, Stiv pleaded, "Please, Vera. I'm sorry. I'm sorry, okay? I was there. I didn't want to hurt Colin that bad. I didn't know it was going to be like that." He let go of me. I could not think. I heard his truck door slam. The engine screamed. I saw the taillights leaving. I crawled on my scraped numb knees. I jolted forward. I ran after those worried running lights glowing scarlet under the dead moon. I ran until I could throw rocks that bounced off his bumper gaining speed. I ran long after I could see him. I ran with giant tears leaking. I stopped in front of an old laundromat. The building was dark. Then Annie was there saying nothing. In her car with the door open. Getting wet in the rain. She opened the passenger-side door silently. She handed me my handkerchief.

"They almost killed him," I said instead of taking it from her.

"I know," she answered. "I know."

I hadn't slept well since Annie got pregnant. Nothing sat right. She would leave David just like Monique. I didn't have a surface brain. My mind was split wide open. I saw my town's mysteries and hidden pockets of strange memory. I had a brain that heard things nobody else did. I saw the armed robbery that turned to violence. I saw Stiv shoot the man in the parking lot of a closed-down grocery store. The blood splattered over broken glass and dried urine. I refused to become hardened to it. I left my mind open.

I stared at images across the street while Annie tried to reason with me inside her car. The ghosts were out in full force. Beautiful La Llorona with olive skin and dark hair sat among wildflowers along the railroad tracks. She wore a white gown. Goldsborough

Creek shuddered and lapped at the clinker pile. La Llorona had eyes of black cast iron—tears of blood made them liquid.

Annie laid her strong, feminine hands on her belly. Her fingertips pushed into her flesh.

Her baby grew. She'd given Stiv a ten-dollar bill. He had nothing. She couldn't help him any more than she could help herself. I was quiet in the passenger's seat. I didn't want to think of her brother shooting a man—a seasonal worker from Mexico. A man who picked salal and sword fern for the tourists' flower arrangements. A man who picked mushrooms for yuppies in Seattle to eat. A man who did not speak English and wired money home to his family. A man who would not start a union or organize a strike. A man as desperate as desperate could be. Who yearned for the smell of chuparosa and hot creosote. Annie drove to Hoodsport and back to help us think.

I saw La Llorona again. She was thin and shaking—walking in the wrinkles of darkness and rain on the side of Highway 101. She stood against tree trunks and garbage cans. The Skokomish River despaired. She picked through trash around tweaker pads. She didn't ask for help. Her eyes were weary yet still bled tears. Her clean dress was gone. She wore soiled rags.

Annie said that I needed to eat—that I wasn't doing so well. Her words bounced around inside my skull that felt broken. I was anemic and drinking too much coffee. Each time I closed my eyes I saw the vapors of gray mist rise from the smokestacks at the abandoned lumber mill downtown. When I opened them I saw the moist, black sky filled with steam. The dampness made the clouds hover. The wavering, coiling billows made things reflect wrong. Figures showed up through the car window even while there was nothing there. "We need to eat and then get some sleep," Annie insisted. She sighed and was exasperated. "Vera, you're so *sensitive*!" I held on to that.

We went to the All Night Diner. Annie tried to get me to eat pancakes heaped with strawberries. It was supposed to be our one night out. Just us girls. My mouth tasted like metal. I couldn't stop thinking. Stiv shot a man and watched his body bleed. Annie was having a baby and none of us could pay our rent. Colin didn't act the same as before his skull was bashed in. He was slow and lethargic. His arresting, high-strung intelligence was damaged beyond repair. It was too much—too many hard things. I heard Stiv's heavy boots walking through maple leaves in crisp, autumn air. They were running through an empty parking lot at midnight. They were coming closer—sneaking up at my back. I turned around. There was nobody in the shabby restaurant but us. The ripped green carpet was bare. The waitress smoked a cigarette and stared at us. I tried to explain myself to Annie but floundered. I felt the dark clouds racing toward us—the machine with motor oil–blood dripping. The words wouldn't come.

Annie said she was taking me home. Her eyes were beyond worry. She drove to the studio apartment I shared with Jimmy James. I watched for La Llorona more earnestly with both hands tensed on the glass. I knew La Llorona was embodied hurt. A deep sadness. Somewhere, a woman was feeling something so strongly I could see La Llorona with my eyes. That man had a wife. In Mexico. That's why La Llorona came and went—I saw her through miles of river water and darkness.

I floundered to explain something to Annie. "It's a stabbing feeling. It squeezes and then lets go. It takes over my whole body when I breathe. It throbs and then comes back. I feel helpless like a little kid. All I can do is curl up in the dark."

Annie didn't answer. She shook her head but didn't say a word.

14

DUANE

I watched the day that Duane took his younger brothers and sisters out to dinner. He just got paid and wanted to buy them all cheeseburgers. They didn't get treats very often. The excitement radiated out of them. It spilled from their bright eyes and wriggling bodies. Nine little kids all in darned clothing. Eighteen small hands clasped patiently. Their oldest brother had an *employee discount*. He had a *job*. Duane carried a tray of water cups to them. He didn't have enough money to buy them all sodas. But they didn't mind. It didn't matter. It felt like the end of all hard times. How could they want *more* when there were ten cheeseburgers all piled onto a plastic tray? The ten warm bundles with bright orange wrappers took over all their thoughts. All their dreams.

Then Duane surprised them: there were *French fries, too*! It was too much. Too, too much. There was another plastic tray holding five paper packages of golden, fried potatoes. They would share with each other. The food was perfect. Duane sat back and watched the second-oldest say grace politely and carefully. They were silent and thankful—filled with wonder. They closed their eyes and tasted. Duane smiled and smiled. They would sleep soundly in their beds that night—remember everything with awe.

Duane had short black hair and a baseball cap. He wore cut-off pants—the ragged edges brushed against his knees. He plodded amiably when he walked. I looked at him closely in the fast-food restaurant. He was different from us Cota kids—softer, more idyllic and hopeful.

Country and dirty. But wiry and strong. Strong as strong could be. He had apologetic, nonviolent muscles. Calloused hands. Just poor, poor, poor without being angry. A hardworking poor boy who dreamed simple dreams. A cabin. A wife. Clean rivers where there were still fish. His soft-spoken words made me look at him shrewdly. He was shy. His eyes were brown. I thought that he could not be real. His hands were tan and gentle. I did not understand how he could be so strong and not wear it on his sleeve like a badge of grave courage.

Duane came down from his mom's little farm in the hills for good when the land got too expensive. It was around the same time Jimmy James came to Cota Street seeking work. Duane wanted to help his mama pay her taxes and keep their land. His two younger brothers were finally old enough to milk the goats, gather eggs, pick berries, chop firewood, and slaughter chickens and pigs themselves.

And besides, Duane was tired of his homeschool books. He thought it was foolish to work so hard just to get by. He wanted to meet people. He was lonely. His mama understood more than he knew. She helped him fill out his job applications. They looked up certain words together in the family dictionary. They printed them out carefully in the spaces provided.

Duane wore handmade flannel shirts. He ate homemade cracked-wheat bread. His mama did the best she could. She was young herself. They lived in a place that didn't have a name—a few scattered cabins with dirt floors, hovels of fifth-wheel trailers. No school. No books that weren't church books. No music that wasn't church music. Trips to town were few and far between. Duane was tired of the miles and miles of dirt roads and trailers and everybody knowing everybody else's business. As Duane got older, he didn't think his mom was fooling anybody with her church and her Bibles. He thought about what it had been like before his father left them with the smell of burnt gunpowder. He remembered everything—the cash crops, the frequent visitors. High schoolers and hippies from the state college dropping by. Day in and day out. People looked twice at him now. They knitted their eyebrows. His accent was strong. To everyone on Cota Street, his words sounded garbled. Duane was not clueless. He knew his destiny—his permanent place in society. The gut feeling was imprinted inside his belly. It wouldn't go away. No matter how hard he tried, his words were always mispronounced. He was outdated. As country as country could be. And country people are wrong a lot.

Duane stayed in a rented room on Cota Street like an animal forced into domestication.

He had instincts hidden inside—but they were soon muted by the asphalt and industrial pollution. He possessed years of hard work and isolation. His senses churned and boiled. He could stalk silently. And kill swiftly. He could work leather and talk to beasts. Duane wanted little from Cota Street. He couldn't help but feel that everything within the city limits was more complicated than it really had to be. He was lost in the fast-food restaurant with the unnaturally bright colors and fluorescent lights—the sour smell of nervous people pressed too closely together. His skills were confused and without aim. He remembered his uncle Bill's hunting dogs the year he broke his hip on the tractor and couldn't take them out. The dogs became angry with their dry food. They wanted pain and fresh blood. Instead, they stewed in their pen. They wanted to be wild but they couldn't. They were locked up in barbed wire. Until finally they were shot for hunting chickens.

Duane raged at how his muscles softened. His instincts faded. He worked graveyard.

There was no sun. The kids he worked with teased him. They talked twice as fast as he did. They tried to sell him things he didn't really want. They drove a cruel path right through all his Bible stories. They lent him their CDs. They showed him their magazines. Duane tried hard to keep up. The other boy who worked the fryer talked to him in unending, abrasive monologues. Duane nodded at the right times. The fryer boy did not particularly like Duane. But he was interested in who Duane knew. The nameless communities up in the hills where the best stuff came from.

Duane tried hard to stay away from the cat piss–smelling meth labs. The hungry dogs. The shacks and the tarps. Angry, snaggletoothed old men ignoring sour-faced, skinny women. His heartbroken cousins. But eventually he let the fryer boy take him up there. Out near an old logging camp. Where the clouds hovered low and the trees grew sparse and tall and thick. Duane showed him where to park. They slammed the doors. The fryer boy looked around him at the trees. He furrowed his brows. "Where's the house?" he asked. Duane laughed for the first time in months. Shook his head and started walking. The fryer boy followed. He couldn't have imagined how dark it got back there between the trees. The slough with ducks. The Doug fir so old it saw through him. Too dark for salal or blue huckleberry. Some of the last few mountain devils hovered not thirty miles away. The tension between Duane's shoulders eased. The fryer boy grew nervous and ill. Duane breathed in deeply. His senses awakened to the quiet damp echoes of the forest air. Here, Duane knew, you could not control anything. Fast talking meant nothing. His nostrils flared like a snuffing black bear. He pawed the ground like a rutting bull elk. Here, he did not fear death. It was out of his control. The most moral thing to do was die quickly and quietly. Raindrops splattered off the branches far above. The fryer boy had no choice but to follow the strange boy through the wilderness. Duane's leather boots crunched over the gravel and thudded on soft mounds of moss. The fryer boy twisted his ankle on a fallen branch. His canvas tennis shoe flew off. Duane did not wait for him. They came to a vague trail. The smell of wood smoke hovered. A small cabin hid above a valley with a winter creek. Eight hound dogs found them long before the cousins and uncles. Their howls chilled the fryer boy down to his bones. Duane smiled. The dogs sniffed and wagged. The rifles lowered their aim when Duane called out. The children were let out of the attic. Both Duane and the fryer boy invested their entire paychecks in meth. Duane would rather have bought the black bear rug or a nice new cookstove. Or some of his grandmother's cast iron pots and pans. He liked how the copper kettles glowed against the wood wall of the cabin. But some things were not for sale. His dreams would have to wait. Times had changed drastically.

Back on Cota Street he laid out a line for himself on the table. He snorted it without thinking. Soon, he did whatever was on anyone's table. He sold to whoever wanted some. He was not careful. He had the best hookups out of all the Cota kids. He did everything too fast, too much. He wanted to make up for lost time. He wanted to get out of there as soon as possible. He did not answer the calls from the fast-food restaurant. He paid his rent in twenty-dollar bills.

Even though he no longer worked graveyard he still did not see the light. He started dating fifteen-year-old Kat. Kat who would cook and clean. Kat who was not jealous. Kat who was never mean. Kat who would let Duane ash his cigarette in her lap and not complain. Kat who did whatever he wanted.

Duane became a fast, hard skeleton. He found himself floundering—hitting up against one sensation after another. His flesh burned away. He felt himself as only a cadaver. The Cota kids hurt him without meaning to. They did it out of habit with no regrets. It had been done to them a thousand times before. He learned to be the man his mother wished he wasn't. He acquired the same stubbly, set jaw as his father. The man Duane remembered with patchy, emotional distraction. The smell of a grown man—the hands of a hard worker—a thick chest that was hard and steady.

Duane changed more and more the longer he stayed on Cota Street. His mama despaired.

He felt guilty and cried at weird times. It made the Cota kids laugh. He was socially awkward and didn't like talking out loud. He grabbed the bodies of underage girls—they were not people to him. He wanted something to replace the flesh he had lost. He had sex with them when they were too drunk to say no. He took pictures and showed the other Cota kids. He felt insatiable. He was all mouth—a hunger that sometimes scared him. He needed to prove something he wasn't sure about. He tried to erase the memories. But he still thought of his daddy's shootin' car. His six-year-old self propped up on his daddy's knee. How his father let him hold the gun and aim at the shootin' car. Then a blankness. Then his shut eyes. Then the gunshot.

Duane was frustrated and angry for longer and longer periods. He watched Jimmy James as his moods grew more and more foul. He was angry that his fast-food wages hadn't been enough. That he couldn't support himself. That he didn't know how to do anything but hunt and fish and harvest. He didn't like how Jimmy James walked. How Jimmy James made the transition so smoothly from the hills to Cota Street. People liked him. Jimmy James taught the Cota kids about firearms and Johnny Cash. Jimmie Rodgers sang from apartment windows.

Duane couldn't stand how Jimmy James looked at him as if he were nothing. His gaze swept through him. Or openly glared.

Duane started to look for chances. He wanted to show Jimmy James a thing or two.

Irrevocably.

He found me, Brady, and Jimmy James one morning in a parking lot when the sun had just risen. Jimmy James and Brady were leaning under the hood of our truck. Jimmy James already had his shirt off. We just bought a new battery. Duane came from uptown. He hadn't slept in a week. He was drinking cheap vodka straight out of the bottle. It was wrapped in a brown paper bag. He stopped and stared. He started to talk.

Jimmy James and Brady glanced at him and smirked without answering. They were not as kind as they could have been. They looked too satisfied with themselves—slick and united—like they knew things Duane didn't. Jimmy James belonged to the mechanic's union. Duane tripped over his own feet and weaved while he talked. He smelled strongly of alcohol. Waves of chemical sweat found us on the warm breeze. His words became gibberish in the dusty air—lost in the curdled smell of his breath. Jimmy James looked annoyed. Duane looked desperate. It was then that Annie arrived. With hot coffee for all of us.

Duane looked at her short skirt in the morning sun. He said something he shouldn't have. Her forehead scrunched up in anger. Hot coffee splattered down his front and onto the pavement. Brady dented Fitz's Honda slamming Duane into it. Got real close to his face. Explained that if Duane ever touched Annie he would feed him his teeth. Duane wasn't like the other Cota kids. He'd never been beaten. His body held no memories of broken noses, teeth rimmed in blood, or eyes swollen shut. He hadn't smelled human blood in a long, long time. And in his mind the smell mixed with peat mulch in the warm sun. It came with the silence after a gunshot and crippled him with memories of his daddy going out to the back field. The one that had been plowed up so that the dark soil stood naked and vulnerable.

Jimmy James and Brady did not think about the downfall of the economy. Or the rise of sex abuse and teenage pregnancy. Or news reporters, the war on drugs, and social control. They knew only that things were different. And they might have to rewrite history. They did not think about the new prison built on the wetland. Or all the men locked up there. They were not assessing churches or silenced goddesses. They knew only that to destroy a man was one thing. But to destroy a man and everything he believed in was to destroy the women he loved. And that rape was a part of war. The boys with shaved heads had only one weapon to protect us. That morning, I hid behind Brady and Jimmy James. Their hard, clean bodies stood shoulder to shoulder. I closed my eyes to meet the scent of their aftershave. I realized that I felt safe. And how important it was to feel safe.

Duane slurred and puked. Brady dropped him on the pavement. He took out his brass knuckles and tried them on—just to see if they still fit. He stretched his fingers through them lazily. He would wait for a better time. Jimmy James's eyes grazed over Duane. That distancing, appraising look. He turned his back completely. He shook his head and smiled to himself. He closed the hood of our truck. The battery was hooked up now. Duane stumbled away on wobbly legs. He wanted to be wild but he couldn't. Fresh blood was out of reach. He was locked up in barbed wire.

Duane left the parking lot in a haze. He was feeling dizzy. He couldn't stop the memories. The smell of peat mulch and fresh blood. He closed his eyes and saw the red and black and brown—the sun shining through his eyelids. The light-headedness—the first few seconds of a blackout.

He resolved then in the alleyway, between the deli and a housing project, to buy a pair of black combat boots. He was going to put white laces in them. The blacktop would have to welcome *the New King of Cota Street.*

He closed his eyes. But his mind was not done yet. He remembered:

His daddy was crying. Bending down in the back field. Wailing. Drunk. He had the shootin' gun. But he wasn't near the shootin' car. Duane and his mother ran to him. Their words never made it to their mouths. The pistol was raised. Duane closed his eyes first. Heard the gunshot second.

His daddy had looked at him.

Straight into his eyes before he pulled the trigger. Red-rimmed. Sallow sockets. A pistol falling. Thudding against the red-darkened soil—the suddenly wet peat mulch.

It was a 1911 with a pearl pistol grip.

15

THE BIG CAT

If Colin had known about the big cat, he might not have taken the dirt bike. But as soon as he got out of jail he looked up a rich kid in Olympia who owed him a lot of money. The kid was a politician's son who wanted to be a redneck. Colin waited with him for two hours at a grocery store. He stared at the kid's stiff Carhartt pants. His new Georgia boots. The boy's money never came through. His politician dad was using tough love. The kid started talking in a high-pitched voice. He was coming down and scared—feeling suddenly vulnerable.

Colin said he wouldn't cut him up so bad if he had something to hold on to. He told him about how nicely the kid would fit into the trunk of his Impala. Colin took the bike and told him he was lucky. He took back roads most of the way to David. He rode down 101 under the speed limit. It was his birthday. He had never in his life owned an Impala.

Colin was tired of the tweakers in the tweaker pads—the track marks, stolen guns, and boredom. He went to the house on Cota Street to look for me. It was empty and stared at him. He couldn't remember where my apartment was. A troublesome thought reminded him there was something he was supposed to tell me. He scrubbed at the wall in the kitchen. There was a blood-stain there. He picked at the sores on his face. Some kids knocked on the door, and he let them in. He didn't really remember their names. They had meth and offered him some. As the smoke left his lungs he grew even more confused. He didn't say a word to the tweakers huddled around the crack pipe in the living room. He grabbed his heavy jacket and walked out the back door. He looked longingly at the porch. He jumped on the dirt bike and bought a case of beer at the corner market.

Colin rode all the way up in the hills above the plywood mill. He followed logging roads until he found one that ended abruptly. He was in a turnaround that only loggers knew the use of. He drank his beer and tried to cut kindling for a fire with his pocketknife. He was shaking. He sliced through his skin. Splinters stuck into his flesh. The wound bled angrily. He wrapped his finger in his handkerchief. The blood soaked through the cotton. He watched the thickets of salal and Scotch broom change shape in the dark. His good-looking face was haggard—saggy bags of dark flesh hung underneath his eyes. Stringy, greasy hair clung to his face. He wouldn't sleep that night or the next. It would take a lonely eternity for the drugs to leave his system.

A mountain lion smelled the fresh blood of his wound. He heard her screeching as he stared at the sun sinking behind a freshly shorn hill. The big feline was young and starving. The sunset ended quickly—beet juice dripped down the clear-cut hill-side. There wasn't as much territory as there had been in the past. Mountain lions were territorial. They weren't afraid of people. The sixty-pound cat stalked him loudly. She wanted to know why he had come. She sensed he was weak and foolish. She made low, growling, whoofing noises. Circled him. Screamed like a woman. She would not leave.

Colin threw a burning chunk of wood at her. He was furious and yelled, "Scat!"

But it was no use getting mad at nature. It was too dark to leave. The headlight on the bike was burned-out. He would get lost in the dark woods if he tried to come down the gravel roads on foot. He would spend days surviving off rainwater and blue huckleberries. Even if he remembered the way, it would take him all night and day.

That night he heard strange things in those mountains. He didn't know what was real and what wasn't. The spirits in the woods were older, angrier, more powerful than the ones on Cota Street. They leered. He was an immigrant who didn't belong. A glacier loomed. The monoculture of Doug fir judged him silently. The trees stood in a row. Jagged stumps wallowed in hushed mis-ery. The soil was eroding and depleted. It would only get worse. He'd forgotten water. He was smart enough to know he wasn't as smart as he used to be. His fingertips brushed across his stitched skull. There was a blankness there. He grew frustrated. He'd be lucky to see the morning. His small fire sent out a womblike, red glow. Sparks traveled up toward the black sky and disappeared. The cat was afraid of the flames. He built up his fire and huddled in the glow. His face burned. The flames towered. He wanted

Monique to see the fire as she drove to Montana. His mouth was dry. He choked and lit two cigarettes. Shook his head. Got up and paced. Shivered and cried like a baby.

The big cat stalked him all night.

16

WHAT IT USED TO BE

The city cops found Duane overdosed in an alleyway with heroin in his pocket. They chose that opportunity to unleash the slew of charges they'd been saving up. His whole family waited at the courthouse for his turn to plead in front of the judge. *His whole family.* All those kids lined up on one of the long benches. The benches that used to be church pews—hand-me-downs from the Baptists. Duane's mom was in her Sunday best. All the girls had braids in their hair. All the boys had short-sleeved, hand-sewn cotton shirts. Everything was ironed and clean. Checkered and corduroyed. Their hair was combed to the side. Duane's mother had a patient look in her eyes. She was praying. She'd been praying for so long it was a constant companion. It was like breathing. She prayed while cleaning house, cooking dinner, and picking berries. Her lips moved faithfully while tilling soil or planning lessons. At the courthouse her prayers reached a crescendo—her eyes and mouth clenched shut. Her posture tense and worried. Her oldest son slouched in handcuffs. There was no place to leave her children. No lawyer. She'd been trying to save money. She sold her wedding ring and placed the cash devotedly into her jewelry box. She was as lonely as her son had been. No friends. She was far away from courthouses and Cota kids and little girl prostitutes with wild, angry hearts.

The charges followed Duane around for a long time. Nobody wanted to buy or sell to him anymore. He was marked. He couldn't get financial aid. Colleges didn't want him. Businesses with benefits wouldn't hire him. He got back on at his fast-food job. But the court system was vicious and tricky. Once he was in, he was in—for life. His schedule became one hearing after another. Sentencing, biding time, waiting around in courtrooms— the horrible, stuffy, nervousness of those places. Everyone was strained. Everyone was pissed. All the men in suits were tired of dealing with people like him. He was just another face—another number. He got yanked around. Court dates changed at the last minute. It took longer than expected. He had no choice. He waited. His fast-food job became a behind-the-scenes thing. He had to take too much time off work. His boss lost patience. People talked. He got fired.

Duane was seventeen when he started hearing voices. Maybe the pressure finally got to him. Or maybe it was going to happen anyway. Either way, he stopped going to his court dates. He ate nothing but soft, raw vegetables from the food bank. He didn't make a lot of sense when he talked. He found God, spoke in tongues, went into trances, and quit bathing. He saw things.

He and Kat got evicted. They visited his mama who cried.

They got a ride back in from the hills with two hunters who dropped them off downtown near the train tracks. Kat found some kids she knew buying cheap wine at the grocery store. She and Duane followed them home.

Duane filled a coffee cup with gasoline and lit it on fire. He woke the kids sleeping in the cheaply rented building with a spoken premonition. The flames dripped down to the floor. They crawled across the thirty-year-old carpet. Duane rambled and gestured violently. "I know God is real!"

There was a deep blackness to the night. The flames reflected in his eyeballs and metal facial piercings. The Cota kids were excited and laughing. They crawled out of their cocoons of thin blankets and clothing. They rose from their mattresses, stood up from couches, emerged from the floor. None of them had to go to work in the morning. There *were* no jobs. They laughed because Duane was back. The building they lived in was burning to the ground. The destruction of the old I.W.A. meetinghouse would barely be noticed. The mural of the union seal on the side was now curled and blistered paint. The tweaker neighbors in the Section 8 housing across the street were busy with their own tasks behind thin, cheap walls. The Cota kids knew they were young and fucked over. Their lives would happen without anyone noticing. They laughed and laughed. Nothing had ever *been* so funny. They danced in the street and watched the fire blast out windows—send licks of orange-tinted radiance into the sky.

Duane stayed downtown on random couches after that. His brain flew away like a tired bird. He started to jog. He jogged in parks and on hard pavement. He jogged during the day, and he jogged at night. Same old shoes. His hair grew into long, natural curls. A broad, swaying beard sprung from his face. His forehead and eyes peeked out from the shaggy mane. His clothes grew tattered and faded. His body ate itself—the exercise waned his strength. His frame formed even thinner lines. His eyes hollowed, and his bones were wire.

Duane was filled with a useless mixture so volatile it seethed through his pores and into the foggy David night. He proved that the news reporters and tourists and college students and police officers were right. We were just as bad as bad could be. For no reason. His actions were exhaled cigarette smoke being swept into a vent. His life was an empty milk carton rotting—a CD too scratched to play. His heart turned into a discarded coffee cup harboring enamel blistered from flames—smelling strongly of gasoline—so black from the soot left by fire no one could tell what it used to be.

17

A BAD STATE

Something about the way Kat tripped coming up the front steps got to me. Her head flew up in fear at the loss of balance. She grappled for the railing that leaned. She was wide-eyed and saw me watching her through the window. Her face showed a brief glimpse of infuriated loathing. Then a painful effort at control in the evening light. I felt a stab of pity—a deep hopelessness that paralyzed.

I knew Duane must be in a bad state to send Kat to us. She scuttled awkwardly across the front porch. She'd never been to Brady, Joey, and Fitz's trailer before. She looked around the front porch. Her sharp gaze rested for a moment on the river rocks that lined the dirt pathway—proof of a resident feminine presence. She filed away that piece of information and knocked rapidly on the front door. It was just before dusk on a Sunday. The Douglas fir quietly draped themselves in shadow. The moon had already risen. Soon, stars would blink between the treetops.

Because of how she tripped, I didn't warn Fitz, who answered her knock and let her inside. Her glance flitted quickly from one body to another: Brady. Annie. Fitz. And the Man from Angel Road. All standing there. Mouths agape. None of us spoke to her. She didn't make eye contact. She rubbed her thumb against her forefinger. Up and down. Up and down. Kat glared at my chest last. Her gaze rested there.

She was stooped and bland and gibbon-like. Hunched shoulders. Fine hair. Her eyes were blank yellow dots surrounded by thick lines of black eye makeup. Her juvie tattoos were splattered unevenly on her skin. The lines were irregular—the ink blotchy and fading. Kat was short and compact. Even though she wanted to be swift and nimble. Her feet tripped. But she was still more like predator than prey.

Kat squirmed past Fitz and sat on the floor in front of the coffee table with her legs crossed. She pulled out a shapeless bundle from inside her jacket and carefully unwrapped a heavy pistol. Set it down on the table with both hands. Told us it was for sale. We stared at her. She fingered the metal like a lover. Like her world depended on the steel. Brady knelt down in spite of himself. Took it carefully out of her fidgety fingers. Examined it closely.

"A 1911," he mumbled in soft awe.

"With a pearl pistol grip," Kat finished proudly. She almost smiled. Her clean, beige hair was tucked behind her ears—it curved around her chin.

Jimmy James looked at them both in horror.

"I'll take whatever I can get," Kat assured Brady.

I knew Brady felt sorry for her. Kat's story circled my head. Each detail was hard to swallow. I didn't know her. I knew only the reputation she had gained on Cota Street. I didn't know if she had been born Caitlin or Kathleen. She was just Kat. Her full name was lost on a birth certificate in a drawer somewhere. A drawer that had been rooted through a thousand times in search of valuables to pawn. The family pictures were mixed up and out of order. The files and documents were dog-eared. She was just Kat. An animal name shortened for the convenience of others. She failed high school, alternative high school, and then beauty school. Kat's mom loved heroin more than she loved her daughter who was small and pretty and promiscuous. The counselors at the drug rehab center and volunteers from the state college tried to name Kat's problems. They said words like *severe economic and social depravation.* And tried to measure her life on graphs. They called hers a world of "rural poverty" and other things. But Kat knew better. She had a knowledge that blotted out all those words: *Kat knew she could never be like other people.* And that was all that really mattered.

Brady offered her three hundred dollars for the gun. Her eyes grew bright. She agreed without bartering. She watched him carefully as he went to his bedroom without looking at any of us. He closed the door carefully. Came out with cash. Kat thanked him again and again. For some reason there was a moment of peace. Kat picked up the T-shirt that had once held the gun. She coiled it into a tight ball and stuffed it back into the pocket of her leather jacket. She drew a box of bullets from another pocket—shoved them at Brady.

"They go with the gun!" She grinned graciously.

Jimmy James sat down cautiously on the couch next to Brady. He picked up the revolver and held it close to his face. He shook his head. His eyes finally softened in genuine admiration. He took out five bullets one by one and loaded them gently into the chamber. Kat's eyes watched his fingertips lovingly. She was still grinning eerily.

"That's a steal," Jimmy James told Brady. Then he looked up and saw Kat staring at him as if he were a young and hostile Jesus. He shivered. His face grew dark and dangerous. "Sell it as soon as you can," he advised Brady. The hairs were standing up on the back of his neck. He couldn't shake a bad feeling.

Kat waited until everyone was quiet and uncomfortable and waiting for her to leave. She stared at Jimmy James—past his right shoulder at the fake wood paneling of the trailer. I started to wonder if the chicken breasts I put on the grill were burning. Kat sniffed the air as well. But the scent she was searching for was not burnt meat. She wanted to smell the Man from Angel Road. Her attraction was that of an animal: *pheromones and curiosity and violent timidity—the adoration of an alley cat.*

The thought crossed my mind that cats sometimes kill things just to play with them. They toss mice half alive and squirming into the air—pretend they are still moving—slaughter them over and over.

Kat's eyes grew foggy and haunted. She'd been thinking about this moment for a long time. She stood, reached into her jacket again, and pulled out a spiral-bound notebook. It was black and well used. She held it out to Jimmy James but he did not take it. The pages flapped sadly in the air. She finally set it on the coffee table and pushed it toward him. He looked down at it warily and asked, "What is it?"

"My notebook," she answered. "Where I write things." She was urging him. Begging him. It grew hot in the crowded room of the little trailer. Annie came to stand next to Brady. I felt queasy. "I wanna belong to you," Kat blurted out. "I'll do whatever you want." She stared right at the Man from Angel Road. Fitz turned around to find my gaze. His eyebrows were question marks. I shrugged. Brady's arms searched for Annie's waist. Annie took his hands and pushed them against her distended belly.

Jimmy James looked up at Kat fiercely. Incredulous. With raised eyebrows. It was the first time any of us had ever heard her want something for herself.

Annie tried to be nice. She began tentatively, "People don't *belong* to other people, Kat."

I saw the Man from Angel Road sneer. I saw his face crease into a dark look I had never known before. "Why would I *own* you?" he asked Kat as he scowled. "You're not *worth* anything."

Annie tried. She tried to stop everything from happening. "Jimmy," she pleaded. "You stop it! She doesn't mean it!"

Jimmy James Blood barely waited for Annie to finish. "Yes she *does*! She does mean it!" He shook his head. "Don't you *see*? Don't you see how *she* makes it harder for *you*? How people like *her* make it so hard to get people together, to listen to each other? She's a puppet of this capitalist system, and I don't want *racists* coming to this house anymore! That's final." He was tired and more tired. It was all wearing him down. He was as close to desperation as I had ever seen him. Annie was seven months along.

He worried about me who worried about Colin. All our names were on a list. The files were in a file cabinet. The uniformed men discussed us like a rat problem. There were red arrows pinned on a map pointed right at us. It was inevitable. Our addresses, license plates, and hangouts were on file.

He stood and towered over Kat. He pointed at her. "*You* are on drugs all the time. That's why you're talking crazy like that. Don't you be bringing no drugs or crazy ideas into this house. Do you *hear* me?"

Kat cringed and said nothing.

"You want me to tell you how to live? Is that it?"

Kat wouldn't look at him. Her face was a pale stone.

"Clean *up*! Stop *prostituting* yourself! Walk a *straight line*. Read a few *books*. Do it for yourself. Do it for a long, *long*, time." He turned his back on her. He let his words cut like shrapnel. He let the silence settle around her like the ghost-dust after a bomb—the powder that comes to rest on all the bodies and broken buildings.

Kat had a swastika tattoo. A bad history. That evening, there was no time for languish or therapy. The clock ticked unmercifully. I looked around at our group. We were frustrated teenagers. Fitz kept looking wide-eyed at me. Jimmy James kept staring at the squirming girl. He finally exploded, "I can't *save* you!" He was a storm you just had to let blow over.

Kat looked up and saw us all staring. Her eyes filled with childlike, all-encompassing rage. A raw antagonism. The words were salt in open wounds. Her anger and hurt erupted in a sinister cyclone. Her arms pointed at the ends into hard little fists. Her face lost its halo of fogginess.

"I'll *kill* you!" was all that she said. She glared right at Jimmy James when she said it. High-pitched—in a cat's yowl. The words echoed in my brain. I heard her screeching on St. Louis nights: *I'll kill you*. It bounced back at me like a mountain lion's howl: *I'll kill you*. It was a promise: *I'll kill you*. The words made me shiver.

But the Man from Angel Road had spoken. There was no arguing. He stalked out of the living room. Slammed the hollow back door. I watched his long shadow from the porch light as he lit up a cigarette.

Kat trembled in her ratty Converse shoes and stared at me— the one who watched her trip and fall. She looked at Annie and me in an accusatory way. "Vera Violet *O'NEEL!*" she shrieked. "Annie *KISS!*" She flung her gaze angrily from one of us to the other. We had whole names. First and last. Names and bodies and souls that belonged to us. My sweaty hands found the back of her neck. I didn't think about it but pushed her toward the door. She spilled across the carpet flailing. Screamed and howled as if my touch were burning her. I kept pushing her. She was small and frail. I thought about how Colin wandered in and out of the kitchen on Cota Street. Kept assuring me the stains were still there. He splattered bleach across the spot on the wall that had been painted with Monique's paintbrush—tried to obliterate the mark where his head was used as a palette.

Kat rolled once down the front steps. Found her feet at the bottom and brushed the dirt from her jeans. She didn't turn around. She swished her hips haughtily down the worn dirt path. Kicked at the river rocks. I watched in awe as she scampered along the wooden fence and dove into bushes and shadows. She moved so quickly and with such agitation that I did not notice the square corners of Annie's small diary in the front pocket of her sweatshirt—stolen from the corner of the coffee table where Annie had left it in a moment of distraction. She took it right in front of our eyes—a true thief. Fitz laughed nervously behind me. I watched Kat's stooped running.

I turned to Fitz after Kat was out of sight. I told him the chicken breasts were done, drew his pack of cigarettes from his front pocket, took a bottle of reservation wine from the pantry, and locked myself in Brady and Annie's room with Kat's notebook. I curled up in their bed.

Nobody disturbed me for a while.

Kat's writing was hectic and filled with underlines and words all in caps. The pages had mostly been torn out. There was only one story she wanted the Man from Angel Road to read. I drank a long swallow of cheap blush and closed my eyes before I began reading Kat's words:

> I was 12 when I left. The age eleven had been a word—steady and lyrical, gorgeous with the hills and valleys of a woman. It was sensuous to say. It rolled off my tongue—<u>eleven.</u> When my age turned my life took a nosedive. 12 is a number—a 1 and a 2. It is uneven and the 2nd half is ready to fly away from the rest at any moment. 1 and 2 have so little in common.
>
> I got kicked out of school because I stopped talking after my birthday. It made my teachers shiver—they didn't like to think of why I would stop talking like that. I bought a ticket to Portland with a fistful of stolen

twenties. I traveled south in the half-light of summer. It was when I was 12 that I started saying <u>you</u> instead of I.

I wanted to be somewhere else. So I could breathe and be clean. Not feel sticky in my sheets in my tiny room without a door. I needed a door with a doorknob and a lock. I wanted one so badly. So I could lock myself in. And lock other people out.

He watched me walk up the steps of the bus. The only seat open was in front of him. The bus started moving. The sun was setting. I had to sit down. He wore clean clothes—a suit and tie. He was a businessman taking the bus. He talked sweetly with me about books, authors we both loved. He made me believe in magic. He let me borrow some of his. Male-endowed power. Suit supremacy. Business-lingo authority. He was entitled. I thought he would entitle me, surely.

He could see inside me, underneath my clothes, what happened in my bedroom that wasn't private. HE KNEW! Back then I was alive and angry—I still used <u>Is</u> instead of yous.

SAVE ME, I said with ruined, hopeful eyes. I was stupid. How could he know Kerouac and James Joyce and Walt Whitman and be bad? The shame burned all over—everywhere I looked. HE enjoyed it. HE was just like all the rest. HE liked the pain and devastation of my skinny, hunched shoulders.

HE said, "take a look at those yellow-brown eyes. You're a little Lolita if I ever saw one."

LOLITA!

I shivered and just kept shivering all over. My heart beat faster. I closed my eyes and tilted my head so it rested against the window. HE wouldn't let me sleep. HE knew too much. Too many secrets. He was THE SECRETS MAN.

Clara always said I was "like an alley cat you never really owned." Clara said yous instead of Is. She made herself not a person—she took away her responsibility. She would say,

"You do so much for her! She makes it IMPOSSI-BLE for you to love her!" Clara wanted me to do those things I was tired of doing. That stuff my step-dad wanted me to do.

I told her "I sure as HELL didn't ask to be born." And I meant it. I said I without feeling bad. I was Kat—a person. Clara doesn't love me when I don't do what my step-dad tells me to.

I learned to shut my eyes very tightly when I obeyed—when I "helped them out." I listened to the rain on the roof. The neighbor's tabby sometimes stared at me through the curtains on the window.

THE SECRETS MAN made me drink whiskey with him. He told me to. He pushed a flask toward me and his fist had 2 pills in it. I took the flask from him. I swallowed the pills. I knew all about whiskey. I wanted it so I could sleep on the bus and ignore his eyes looking at me.

The whiskey was like the bile at the back of my

throat that came up afterward. Clara always made a nice breakfast for me. Breakfast even if it was the middle of the day! Clara forgot everything that happened in between her fixes. The only times that were real for her were the times before and the times after. Each after was a bright new day. The time for breakfast. She made pancakes that caught in my throat—pancakes from the mixes that the church gave us. I didn't want to eat the breakfasts and Clara always yelled at me to do it anyway. UNGRATEFUL! she would scream. "She's always ungrateful!" Clara usually washed my sheets and then went to the bedroom with my step-dad. They stayed back there for days on end. Depending on how much I was worth that time. It was less and less as I got older and the number of men grew. And they got more and more desperate.

I swallowed that whiskey all in one gulp. I kept his flask—I shoved it into my backpack.

Because I was an alley cat that was impossible to love.

Sometimes I think about the library that I used to go to when Clara and my step-dad were not sick in the back bedroom. The library didn't have the shadows that my house did. I could read there. When I was on the bus I thought about that library. I closed my eyes to remember exactly what it looked like. The alcohol on my stomach fuzzed my brain. I hadn't eaten all day. I thought those pills were going to burst my heart. I felt the bus move back and forth slightly on the highway—the long stretch of I-5. I could feel the red-rimmed eyes on me and a hand on my leg.

My dreams turned to twin blades of grass. I imagined I was in a Tolkien novel. I always wondered why I couldn't be an elf or a hobbit or something else small and pure and happy. My dreams got weird. I slid down a very thin tip of velvet grass. I slithered into black water. I grew thick along with the grass. I sped up as the blade tilted. I hit bottom. I thought about where I <u>was</u> and where I <u>should</u> be. No one place was safer than the other. I slipped up on the other end of the grass blade. It was like a roller coaster. It did not end. It was a circle that went around and around. It moved me. Then it was only the gentle swaying of a bus. My horrible body and the wind. I was blown around by the poetry of the Secrets Man. He was talking about grass with roots of dark gelatinous water, roots that collected underneath the earth. I felt like I lived there in the dirt. With the pools that looked like bitter, brown syrup. The acid that ate into me when it touched me. I thought that I must be Gollum instead.

Then I realized I was only a sullen, human girl who tempted poor men like the Secrets Man. I felt sick from the Jack and pills. I opened my eyes and saw the lights of Portland reflect off the raindrops running down the glass against my face. I went with the Secrets Man because I didn't have anywhere else to go. My money was gone from my pocket. I couldn't fight him to get it back. Nobody would have believed that he stole it. And the cops would have made me go home or locked me up. I knew what I was getting into. I helped him out for two months before my step-dad found me. He showed up with shaky hands and a stupid .22. He took me back. I kept running away and the cops kept bringing me in. Finally, when I went after my mom with that butcher knife they put me in juvenile detention in Chehalis. I ran away from there, too. But Clara stopped looking for me.

I quit reading after that. I don't fuck with fantasies no more. I forgot all the words I used to know. I started saying <u>you</u> instead of I.

<u>You</u> just can't win. <u>You</u> gotta do what you gotta do.

I felt deflated after reading Kat's words. I got up and paced around the bed. I felt like puking. Annie heard me bumping into things. She knocked gently. I let her in, and she looked at the floor. I couldn't bring myself to destroy Kat's story in the wood-stove as I had planned. Just how Brady couldn't stop himself from buying the pistol. And Fitz hadn't stopped Kat from crossing the threshold into the trailer. I handed the notebook to Annie. I didn't say anything.

Kat disappeared with the money she stole from Duane's ma-ma's jewelry box (six hundred dollars in total from the pawned wedding ring and grocery money). Plus three hundred dollars from the stolen gun and box of bullets. She vanished with no story. Nobody looked for her.

18

BREMERTON

Kat rented a room in a brown-and-white house that tumbled down a steep hillside overlooking the sound. Across the water: *Seattle*. She could hear seagulls and smell the oily ocean water. During the day, she crouched in the dark corners of her room and stayed hidden. She tried to walk the straight line Jimmy James told her about. But she had trouble. She started out with a simple, dead-end job and cleaned up for a while. But her hands shook with anxiety. Her mind thought crazy thoughts. She couldn't quit hooking. There was no explaining and no one who listened. She had no friends. She couldn't stay clean. But she swore there would be no more crazy stuff. No more meth or crack. She became a closet junkie. Like suburban jocks. A bedroom addict hiding pills instead of needles. It was easier. She drank more than she would have had there been friends around. She drank and drank—became more bitter and lucid as her lonely intoxication grew. She planned to come back to David after a long, *long* time.

She would show him.

Thoughts of the Man from Angel Road boiled her blood. Made everything in front of her indistinguishable—tinted red from her terrible, frenzied fury. The navy boys thought of her as a dumb, shy, country girl. They felt sorry for her. Gave her cigarettes and wine and cocaine. They told her things they wouldn't have told anybody else. They thought she didn't understand most of it. They dumped all their garbage out—made insidious confessions of things they had done.

Kat walked home the same way every morning. Ate a TV dinner. The dinners were always the same kind: *One piece of gray meat. A soggy vegetable. Runny, mashed potatoes.* She took her pills—one and a half. Sometimes she smoked them. Sometimes she swallowed them.

She slept quietly, dreamed silently. But she had only one dream in which:

Her pituitary is pumping out strong messages. It is dark and he is asleep. She crawls through his window into his bedroom. She is lithe and sneaky. She rubs her cheek against his skin and claims him. She is sinewy. Dark. Graceful. She moves gently against him—breathes in his scent. She noses at his armpits, his groin—where the hair holds the strongest odor. Inhales long and deep. Hindquarters in the air, entire body attune.

He stirs and wakens.

He watches with the light off as she crouches in the corner. Her tail twitches. She paces back and forth. She makes low, growling, whoofing noises. Throws her voice. Screams like a woman. He turns his back confusedly to look around—see who else is there. His bedsheets fall from him. His strong lats flex. It is her one chance. She launches herself. Feels the hard plate of her chest hit his back between his shoulder blades. She uses all her strength— her weight. His arms fly out. The wind is knocked out of him.

Her claws dig into his eye sockets, her tail twitches in ecstasy, the muscles ripple underneath her fur, her canines sever his spine.

The taste of blood, the silent struggling, his body slowly collapsing underneath her . . .

Kat moaned in confusion from her dreamworld in her twin bed in her friendless rented room. Nobody heard her. An ambulance rumbled the walls. Its siren sounded long and red into the bustling morning. She stirred only slightly.

She woke trembling from her dream every evening. She cleaned herself in the small, communal shower. Soap that didn't smell good. Cheap, single-blade razors. Her rented room had no windows, so she walked the docks to pass the long, lonely afternoons. The daylight seemed foreign. At Charleston Beach Road she got on the railroad tracks and walked along the water.

She sensed the giant gray ships looming and blinked at the bright lights. She saw all the highway signs with the name of her hometown written on them in reflective white on green. But she did not go home. She waited in the wicked seaport and listened to the sounds of the naval shipyard on the breeze. She watched the steel ships for a sign that crowds of men with shaved heads had commandeered the vessels, made right what had been done wrong, and finally come to save her.

19

THE DANCE OF THE GHETTO

wondered how long I would lie on the camping mat in the windy city. I did not sleep but had strange dreams. I stared numbly at the wall. I read my copy of *Little House in the Big Woods* for fifth-grade reading group. Diamond picked the book out, and I was supposed to make up questions. Diamond told me they had to be *hard questions.*

Outside, there were festivities in Lafayette Park. There was live music and young men reciting poetry. Children danced. Outside, there were messiahs and leaders and priestesses with wide eyes. The Black Panthers marched.

But inside there was dark. There was rest. There was a thin blanket that was my nest. There were coffee cups, books, heat, and quiet. I could hear the sirens and yelling through my walls—but inside I did not even have a phone.

The day before I was at Meadows crouched on the floor—that

same gleaming, golden hardwood floor. The dust and the rat piss. I held on tightly to the six-year-old with dry, scaly patches of skin on his scalp. "It's okay," I whispered with my arms holding tight, rocking as his skinny hands searched for mine. The lights were off. It was black. We heard snuffles and scared murmurs. Tall, bossy Diamond huddled close beside me with giant tears running down her cheeks. I couldn't hold them all.

Eighty-seven children had never been so quiet.

Eighty-seven children and one me. I wanted to put my arms around them all before they tried to scamper out the open door. I slammed it shut. I hoped the thick brick walls would protect us. I hoped the thick brick walls would grow and expand suddenly—to become miles in width—to save us all forever.

It was forty-five minutes until the police came. I pictured the men with guns running the halls—searching for me and my silent children. Every ghetto has its king. Each Cota Street has its own Jimmy James. We all paid homage in different ways. I didn't want the young eyes to see the dead man splayed out on the concrete of the playground—his body filled with holes. Or the Caprice that sped away. The three quick shots in the afternoon. How the blood soaked into the hot blacktop.

Trinise and Marvin were both sorry they had left me alone. They had their reasons.

Trinise: home with a sore throat. Marvin: a visit with Patrice.

I told the principal I was taking a few days off. He shrugged and nodded. He dusted his books with his back to me. "That's fine, Ms. Vera. We will see you soon." He didn't expect me to come back.

I was eighty-seven years old that night in my bathtub. One

year for each child who was caught in the crossfire. It was easy and simple to lie down in my bed. I swam through a thick fog. I escaped. I called for the Man from Angel Road in my dreams. I brushed against him in the night. But somehow, I could no longer remember his face. His voice was either screams or whispers.

When I came back I asked Trinise and Marvin if news reporters had come to Meadows after the shooting. They shrugged. I did not tell them how I disliked news reporters. And that I would escape them at all costs.

Trinise told me, "No one came here, Vera. They never do."

20

BLACK ROCKS

Kat studied Annie's diary carefully. She imagined love. She filled a notebook to replace the one she had given to Jimmy James. She submitted a poem to a literary journal. They sent her a check for twenty-five dollars and a copy of the magazine. Kat never cashed that check. She looked at her name in print often. The poem was on gray-purple paper and read:

Annie Kiss and Hot Rod Brady Robbins
on the Sol Duc

It is hot, and her hair is that color. Her skin is tanned brown. She has swum in the river for 3 days. She has swayed on the sandy banks in the evening. She has let the cold glacier melt wash over her. She is 17. She holds a black rock to her cheek. She tells herself she will never go back there. To that place. To the cold trailer stink and artificial light.

Her hair is braided. Sun-bleached. She has not unbraided it. It has not been combed. For 3 days. She paddles to the river bend. The water flows faster there. It is blue, blue, blue, and deep. She turns over and floats back to him. He is 18. He watches her. He watches his dry fly float on the water. He watches her for longer.

Her pink towel is drying on Japanese knotweed. She pulls it down, shakes it clean, lays it on the bank, studies the snag pile of uprooted trees, and sleeps.

Eventually, he reels in, leaves the fish on a stringer in the cold water. He goes to her, stands close, his drips wake her.

He does not say he loves her. But he sits at her back, unleashes her hair from the barrettes, and combs it tame.

In her notebook, Kat wrote, feeling an anxious dripping sensation in her stomach—an ulcer that burned. In her apartment there were no river rocks. No trees. There was not a gentle, golden hand tugging at stubborn childish braids. There was no brown hair. She lay in her small bed and tried to sleep. But there was no rest. She finally dreamed of things other than Jimmy James. And the nightmares—she ran from them in her sleep. Kicking and screaming. She clawed at them. She kicked her blanket to the floor. She scraped the wall at her head. Bruises colored pale skin. She lay on her back and remembered things. She wanted to tell Annie Kiss, *You can't* be *like other people.* There was a water stain on Kat's ceiling in the shape of praying hands. There was a trail across her floor that she walked when she could not sleep. When she paced, the sound of her footsteps echoed. Slowly, inside those four walls, she withered. Her sad mind concocted a disturbed plan. If there was no room for her back in David, she would make room. It was a stupid idea. But Kat was young. And life had made very few promises to her.

She waited for the night when Annie came to her door in angry tears. Annie didn't know anyone else in town. Her presence and her trouble were like a beautiful gift. Kat knew Annie was too proud to stay on at the clubs. Brady and Jimmy James had tricked her into thinking she was better (the fools). Annie had surely talked back to the owners. Sauced them. Not gone to their parties. Set a bad example for the other girls. The saggy skin of her belly hung angrily. A new tattoo slashed across her left shoulder blade. No cute baby. Annie a junkie. Kat smiled to herself. Annie had old stretch marks on her belly. Kat herself had helped cover them with makeup before she went on stage.

"I'm sick, Kat," Annie said to her in the doorway of Kat's room. Annie was faint and hollow. *Sick*. Annie had a black eye, a bloody nose. "I got fired," she explained. Bloody gravel stuck to her thigh from being drug through the alley. "I need your help," she pleaded. "I'm tired of all this. I wanna go back to David. Will you call Brady?"

"I'll help you," Kat told her after a long moment. She picked up a dingy yellow washcloth from her kitchen counter. Closed Annie's fingers around it. Held it under Annie's bleeding nose. Kat spoke in short sentences. "You stay here. I'll be back. Wait on my bed." Kat shut the door behind her without locking it.

Annie stared at the washcloth. Rubbed tenderly at her face. She crumpled on Kat's bed and watched the yellow cloth turn bright red. She was eighteen.

Kat ran down the hall and up one flight of stairs. Knocked at a door. Got everything she needed. They were used to her there. She bought for her customers often. They fronted her what she asked for and she came back down to her apartment with her pockets full.

Annie was so sick Kat had to shoot her up herself. She'd done it before—different elbows and skins. She was good at finding veins in unlikely places. Peering intently. Poking and prodding. Annie protested at first. "No more!" she wailed. She wanted to clean up bad—wanted it more than Kat had ever seen. Kat shook her head. *Pride again*. It would be Annie's downfall.

Kat reasoned with her firmly, "It's bad for you to go cold turkey. It's too hard on your body. I'll just give you a little bit so you aren't sick. You need methadone." A spot of blood appeared where she slid the needle out. She put a piece of cheap toilet paper on the tiny wound. The blood seeped onto the tissue and stained it red. She put it in her pocket. Annie's eyes rolled back into her head. She'd given her more than *a little bit*. A pool of urine darkened the blanket beneath her. Annie was flailing and groggy and sick and out of control. Kat carefully pulled the washcloth out of Annie's hand. She put it in her pocket next to the bloody tissue paper. Closed the door to her apartment and went out to the street. She walked to the end of the block and used the pay phone to call Brady. The sea wind brought the scent of dead marine life. She had the phone number memorized.

It was an important day. The day the Man from Angel Road borrowed Fitz's Honda to drive to Bremerton. He listened to the CD player—Mark Lanegan sang about shooting little Sadie down. He wore fourteen-eye oxblood boots and black Levi's, a black flight jacket and a black skullcap. He was in a good mood. He didn't mind being tired the next day. He was going hunting with me in the morning. But he could sleep all afternoon. It was only ten dollars in gas to drive to the navy base in the little Japanese car. He had accomplished quite a few things in Seattle that day. He took the ferry back to Bremerton to meet with some friends and change his clothes.

Brady told Kat he was on his way to work. He'd been on graveyard for six months now. He told Kat where Jimmy James was. Brady was tired and not thinking too clearly. "Catch a ride back to David with him. Call me at work if you need me. I'll be home in the morning. I'll leave the back door unlocked." Brady was in danger of losing his job. He'd taken too much time off already. He was sleepy—had been working overtime—eleven straight weeks—twelve-hour shifts—an hour commute each way. No weekends. His bed was lumpy and caving in. The extra money he earned would put him in a different tax bracket. He lost most of it. He worked the overtime to keep his job.

Kat trotted contentedly down the intermittently lit street. She smiled smugly. Her room was still unlocked. She didn't worry about anybody coming in and hurting woozy, vulnerable Annie Kiss. She cut through an alley. She moved closer to the Man from Angel Road. She knew exactly where he was. She knew exactly who he was with. Duane told her about friends and enemies.

How you had to keep your friends close. And your enemies closer. She ran past the docks and through the mist. She pounced on a fallen quarter that gleamed in a streetlight.

She burst into the concert house on a mission. It took quite a while to talk Jimmy James into the alley where he could hear her words. He stood reluctantly while she talked. He sighed and thought it over. He said good-bye to his friends without explaining.

The drive back to David was silent. Kat was content in the backseat holding Annie's head in her lap. Jimmy James pretended that he was alone. When they got to Brady's he carried Annie into the bedroom. When he came back to the car Kat was gone. The hair stood up on the back of his neck. He went back into the trailer and crouched down next to Annie's head. He talked softly and rapped at her temple.

"Annie? You still in there?"

She smiled in spite of herself and pushed his finger away. "Fuck off! Go bother Vivi and let me die here, alone, thank you." She buried her face in the pillow.

"You know, Ms. Kiss, I think you will live," Jimmy James answered. He took a bottle of sleeping pills from the medicine cabinet and set them on the nightstand. He gave her a glass of water. "You'll need these," he said. After hesitating, he took the .45 from underneath the pillow on Brady's side of the bed. He took the ammunition from the top shelf of the closet and sat down to load the gun. He pushed each bullet in tenderly. "Just in case," he told Annie. "This will be here. Underneath the mattress on your side. Got it?"

She moaned unintelligibly.

He told her Brady would be there soon and shoved the gun under the mattress. "It's loaded, okay?" He nudged her.

"Oh-*kay!*" She glared at him and sweated. Then she sighed. "Thanks." Tears pooled in her eyes. "I'll see you guys when I feel better. Send Ms. Violet my best regards."

He nodded and strode away. Annie heard him lock the front door and then the sound of his truck rumble to life out front. When all was silent she could have sworn she heard a strange cry and something scratching at the door. She swallowed sleeping pills and lay back on the pillow—exhausted.

The spot of Annie's blood that was on the toilet paper in Kat's pocket was bright red. The blood on the washcloth next to it was darker—mixed with sparkly makeup and little bits of tar.

The blood that dripped onto the gravel much later that night was shady against the black rocks. A few spots splattered against an old fence post. After a while it turned darker—closer to black. It matched Jimmy James's boots more closely.

PART 3

21

HAIR

My hair was blond and snarled easily. Each strand was fine but it grew thickly over my scalp. It was so straight it did not hold curls. It unrolled from hot curling irons and lay limp. The little girls at Meadows asked to touch it—to put their hands tentatively on the smooth strands of gold. They told me they had never felt anything like it. They asked me why on earth I didn't grow it longer. They told me if they had hair like mine, they would grow it down to their toes.

Diamond named its color cornsilk.

I told them that my best friend Annie's hair had been very long, and it swallowed her like a warm robe made from shiny animal fur. I explained how it had danced upon her shrugging shoulders—how men had stared at it, and baby's fingers had reached toward the shiny piles of brown with greed and adoration.

I told them there was nothing Annie could have done about the attention—it was her mother's hair.

The rising heat and humidity was not good for Diamond's perm—it was growing out.

The ends of her hair were breaking off. Nelly was on tour and sang about "cornrows and manicured toes"—things you were more likely to see in the suburbs unless you had a nice auntie who would do it for free. But Diamond lived at the orphanage six blocks away. She had hair that stood up on end. It became fuzzy. She could not grease it down. She tried vainly but it would not flatten. Her hair was fried and angry—it stood for a struggle she felt in her bones. Always.

Always would her hair betray her. It split from her head in squirming strands. In retaliation, she set her back ramrod straight. With her shoulders steady. And stared at the other children in the homework lab until they looked down in shame—grazing over the parts of her that were breaking.

Diamond was an expert in a certain type of knowledge—her brain stored information that wouldn't get her a high SAT score. She possessed survival skills. She knew how to hide from a repo man. She watched the ladies who ran the orphanage pinch and pull and save and barter and get food and clothes when there were none. Diamond knew how to talk. She was strong. Even when it didn't look good. Even when nothing made sense. She looked around her with shrewd eyeballs that already had the power to terrify grown men. She weighed and calculated. She learned at a young age that sometimes the board games at the orphanage had missing pieces. And so the children made up new rules to make do. But the new rules applied only to the games at the orphanage.

And outside of those rusty gates was a different world. A world where those rules couldn't win. And in that world, Diamond's eyes couldn't save her from harm.

She watched the football game impassively during the after-school program. During slow parts she scribbled in a notebook. She sniffed when one of the fifth graders cried fat tears after the boys from the county with matching uniforms beat Meadows fifty-three to zero. The home team didn't walk with their usual cockiness the next day, or the day after. They tasted a cold, bitter envy at the back of their throats. Diamond tore the page from her notebook and shoved it at me on her way out. It was a poem called "My Hair Is Normal." She gave it to me without a word or a sideways glance. Her nose ring sparkled defiantly. Her arms were certain. She wrote the poem even though there had been no assignments due.

I remembered that small children are capable of great defiance. Defiance that overwhelms. Defiance that changes small worlds completely. Dangerous feelings that blot out everything.

From that point on Diamond wrote. She gave me so many poems I kept a box of them. I told her we would make a book. Diamond wrote a poem, "Cadillac," about how fancy cars rarely crossed the lines onto the crumbling blacktop streets of her neighborhood. And "The County" about how when Suburbans *did* come, it was for three reasons: There were guns for sale. There were drugs stashed. There were sad, pretty ladies who had seen the hardest of hard times. She wrote a fiction piece in which simultaneously a woman with fake nails drank a martini in Soulard, a teenager in tight jeans swallowed OxyContin in rural Illinois, and a housewife from Washington County donated hand-knitted socks to Diamond's orphanage. She wrote and she wrote and she wrote. I kept all the papers carefully flattened and stashed away. We edited and rewrote. I asked Diamond what she wanted to name her book. "*My Hair*," she told me sternly.

The strength of the Northside waned and then flickered. A strange sickness seemed to linger there. The winter waned. I watched the pages of typed text flap in the wind outside the free clinic on Vandeventer Avenue—the names of all the people who tested positive for HIV.

Summer came quickly to the collapsing brick and blacktop.

The sunshine cooked us in our hot-oven schoolhouse. I sweated and grew apathetic. The air was hard to breathe. My lungs ached each morning. A fourth grader at the orphanage died from an asthma attack—Diamond's best friend. Her stony face creased in sadness when she asked me, "Why we always *dyin'*, Ms. Vera?"

I looked out the window at the oak trees and the street in the front of the school. Green leaves waved lightly in the sodden air. Winter was suddenly over. My tongue screamed for cold, clean, unchlorinated water. Unpolluted air. Diamond read out loud in Mrs. Halls's class. She was tongue-tied and stumbling. The words in the book seemed foreign in her mouth. Even Mrs. Halls was sweating.

She told Diamond, "Thank you." Then smiled.

From under her desk she brought out a bright red cooler. Inside were carefully cut-up pieces of chilled fruit. I saw the children's shining eyes. I heard their contented sighs. The vitamin C was just what they needed. It was little things like cold fruit that saved the world.

Mrs. Halls let them talk as they ate. I took a strawberry and a slice of pineapple and said, "Thank you." I graded papers slowly.

Diamond chewed on apple slices and stared out the open window. Her hair was a perfect halo. I looked where her eyes were trained in interest. A 1967 Mercury Cougar with a rattle-can red-and-gray paint job and a dented hood was parked with one and a half wheels on the curb.

I blinked at the lines on the steel body. The vision hit me like a cinder block to the side of the head. My jaw dropped. I moved to sit next to her and stare.

Diamond's gaze drifted toward the burned-down buildings behind the car and Mirabella dancing on Sullivan, then finally to Mrs. Halls who stood in front of the classroom and talked about the field trip to Meramec River on Friday. Diamond passed me a note. On it was written *That's my daddy's car!*

Mrs. Halls showed pictures of rose mallow and buttonbush. She played a tape recording of bird calls: rails, bitterns, and moorhens. She talked about wetlands and prairies and how St. Louis was also called Mound City. I looked at her overhead pictures of mounds covered in wildflowers. Two foolish tears pooled in my eyes.

I took out colored pencils and my sketchbook. I hurried to draw the Mercury Cougar on the street before it drove away. My initial crude pencil lines elaborated into a colorful scene: A crème-colored '67 Merc and a wild-girl driver. A cigarette dangling from fine fingertips. Sunglasses riding a pretty nose. Red lips smirking.

At the center of the scene was the thickest brown hair there ever was. It glinted in summer light. The wind from the rolled-down windows held it up for the mere pleasure of touching it.

Diamond looked over and nudged me. She whispered excitedly, "I want it on the cover! Can I use it please, Ms. Vera?!" Mrs. Halls glared at us both. I nodded and shushed Diamond with eyes that warned, and she turned back around eagerly. I added a passenger to the car: a young girl with old eyes. A pretty girl with skinny arms and a strong chin—hair that was normal. When Diamond was brave enough to look again her face broke into a rare smile. Her back quivered in ecstasy. She scribbled a note on the smallest corner of paper and passed it to me with warm hands. *THANK YOU!!!* was written on it in red marker. Mrs. Halls noticed. She shook her head exasperatedly.

There was no tombstone or memorial for Annie Kiss. But there was a colored pencil drawing on the cover of a self-published book. There was an imaginary ride where two strong girls explored a red desert dotted with giant saguaros and purple prickly pear. They headed toward a hill covered with paloverde and acacia. It was a wet spring. The cactus bloomed.

That night, I attached Diamond's typed and edited poems together. I put a color copy of my drawing on the hard cover. I signed the colored-pencil drawing and placed it in a frame for her.

I thought about all my other drawings and paintings—how they were probably gone now.

I didn't know where. I sat on the camping mat, smoking, and did not sleep.

22

JUNK

I saw Annie's Cougar in the junkyard two days before I left for St. Louis. It was early in the morning. I'd been wandering all night. I came to the junkyard two hours before it opened. But through the fence I saw the Cougar between an Econoline and a one-ton truck. A coil of rusted chains sat above the driver's-side window. They bled from the rain. Rivulets of oxidized red slid down the body and collected along the fenders. But I knew it was Annie's because the paint job was one of a kind.

The car was wrecked—the beautiful, rosy-beige paint crinkled and split where the steel was bent. The skilled welding was wasted. Its hood yawned open and exposed its nearly empty contents—a skeleton of a belly with no engine. A few hoses and cut fuel lines was all that was left of the carefully rebuilt 289. The radiator was disconnected along with the motor. It sat sadly in the empty cavity under the hood.

I stood outside the gate of the junkyard and stared. It was Annie's mangled heart that huddled among the wreckage.

I took the Grays Harbor Transit to Aberdeen. I got out at the shingle mill and scanned the parking lot for Brady's truck. I searched for the familiar trouble—the hot poker I just could not put down.

I hung out by the lunch truck and smoked menthols. I waited. Inside, Brady was a bleary-eyed ghost who stood in a fog. The mill was dark and dreary. The machinery persistent and loud. He could hear only his own thoughts—and they tortured him. The clock announced 8 a.m.

The men relaxed.

Brady bought cigarettes and orange juice from the lunch truck. I looked at the faded orange lines of the parking lot. The paint was chipping and blistered. The men from the graveyard shift looked sleepy. They smiled. Brady stared at the floor and mumbled to the cashier. He smiled without showing his teeth. I stood in front of the soda machine at the entrance.

Brady stuck his smokes in his shirt pocket and noticeably cringed when he saw me. He stood for a moment with his eyes closed. He gathered his thoughts. His right hand squeezed his orange juice as he walked toward me. He leaned against the soda machine. My reckless fists pounded the plastic buttons on the machine. The other men nodded at me politely. They said nothing as they slipped past us. None of them bought sodas.

"Let's go," Brady finally said. As we walked through the parking lot I told him that Timothy was at Nadine's. Would stay at Nadine's. I told him how Colin's red eyes no longer found mine. And that sometimes he still asked if I'd seen Monique. I rambled on about these things. My words found only the empty cave of Brady's mind.

In *his* brain, Annie was home. She washed and waxed her Cougar. The Galaxie 500 was not wrecked. There were no horrible, blank mornings. The '57 was flat black and rumbled in the garage. And Jimmy James played his Les Paul loud enough for the whole neighborhood to hear.

Brady unlocked his Bronco, motioned for me to get in, and slammed the door behind me.

He got in and let the engine warm up. He stared into the street for a moment. He blinked bloodshot eyes. The world suffocated him. Heavy black plastic smothered his face. It obscured his vision. He took a shallow breath. "I'm glad you came," he said as he maneuvered through the moldy city. He drove home in silence.

When we got there, the single-wide and porch were cluttered. Every space was filled with different projects in various stages of completion. They jumbled together and spilled out onto the bare earth.

Patch panels hid in cardboard boxes. They leaned against the porch out of the rain. They waited to be welded onto the steel bodies. They waited for the careful, feminine hands to do them justice.

Jimmy James's Fairlane waited patiently under blue and green tarps. Its mean front fenders peeked out threateningly. They told cautionary tales about Jimmy James's temper. The younger boys who hung around were duly warned. The fenders were smug. They jeered at everyone but him. They cast insults and bragged haughtily.

But Jimmy James hadn't come to see the '57 lately. The car was bleak and morose. Its tarps were unkempt and forgotten. It sat in the rain and the upholstery rotted. Grass grew through the tires. It stewed and became acidic—flat black and rusty.

I knew the car would change if Jimmy James came near. It groveled and begged for his attention. The metal came alive when he touched it. The '57 waited. It waited for Jimmy James, Brady, Fitz, and Joey to turn up their music, get their tools out, and drink beer. It waited for Annie to put on her mask and weld her fine, perfect lines while casting shadows in the blue light from the flame. It waited for the grease under their fingernails that never quite went away—the black that stained the calloused hands— the blood that smeared unheeded. The metal echoed with the sounds of the laughter and curses that lasted all night. It had a memory of the young kids who showed up in hordes to watch. The pretty girls who spit and swore. The young boys who smoked cigarettes and watched. We all drank vodka straight from the bottle. Annie stood tall and shouted orders. She was thin—loud and direct—murderous if crossed. Kids flocked from machine shops and tattoo parlors in two counties to watch the boys with their shirts off and Queen Annie with her scowl. I sat on a bench out of the way and drew it all: The grease monkeys. The wrench tattoos. The shaved heads. Steel that waited for strong young bodies to crowd around it. To grow smudged and oily and black and bloody from the work. The Fairlane that waited for the Man from Angel Road to spew cuss words. That waited for his temper to flare and take on the world. Throw punches with incurable rage. I drew the wide shoulders that loomed in doorways and helped make possible among us a pure, formidable desire—to make happen all the careful plans that had been laid.

I remembered how I first searched for the name that I fell in love with. How I hunted the streets of a dead town for a live soul. Jimmy James—lit up by a streetlight in the parking lot of the All Night Diner. The night I realized he was the Fighter Boy from so long ago. His shaved head unreformed. A thin strip of hair on his chin. Suspenders with no shirt. Denim and boots. His wifebeater hanging from his back pocket. It was summertime. He was free. His tattoos told stories of worldwide organizations, decadence in peril, letters and numbers and codes and symbols. A 428 sat spewing on a hairless chest. Prone and spluttering. Motor oil like dark blood dripping. He stood on that curb while his Ford Ranger idled. He talked seriously. His body lithe and powerful. Cota kids, country boys, teenagers from the immigrant work camps, and boys from the rez all stood around him. They listened with reverence and wide eyes fixated. He was a livid god. His lips curled and cursed. They slid over crooked teeth. His feet stood shoulder-width apart. His worn jeans clung to him. His hands gestured easily with conviction. The boys spit on the pavement littered with trash. And they listened to him preach anarchy. And they listened with their heads raised. And he spoke of the revolution. And they stood there as every color became one color—the color of life and death.

He talked of the world dissipating and forgetting. Flames from piles of burning books reaching the sky. History being rewritten by evil men. He kept talking with a crazed assurance. About the reason why Joey was in Alaska at the cannery—the reason for the lockbox bolted to the wall underneath Brady's bed—the reason all of us had begun to hold our heads so high. The knowledge that would give us power—that would *save* us.

Our apartment had a door that was opened to agitated sixteen-year-olds. The Man from Angel Road listened while the young men talked lowly and earnestly. He encouraged and supported. I hid under the covers from the hallway light while they talked, and the door slammed, and the engines rumbled outside in the parking lot. Sometimes, he did not return to me in our bed. Those times he leaned down with his jacket on, laced his boots, pulled on his black skullcap, soothed me with anxious whispers, "I gotta go take care of a few things. Promise I'll be back." He told me not to let anyone in, before he locked the door behind him. I gathered Timothy and carried him to the big bed. I held on to his little body and felt like I was in a war zone. I watched his cheeks huff in and out with his breath. My heart yearned to be standing beside Jimmy James, and I wondered if maybe I was a better fighter than Mother.

That day at Brady's, Fitz came home early from his gas station job. He told us he'd been fired. He stared straight ahead and looked bored and angry—explained to Brady and me about how the tourist customers were offended by him. He was not good at being nice. Fitz sat next to Brady on the front porch. They both looked beaten down. It took me to a place beyond misery. I didn't like seeing them with no hope. They didn't look strong anymore—something had punched the wind out of them. We sat in silence. It was Friday. We looked at the fog, and the old evergreen trees, and listened to the neighbor's tractor. We had our backs against the wall, our boots up on the railing. We stared morbidly at the ground. The fence post and the black rocks—the stains from the dried blood. We opened our beer cans in unison. "I saw the Cougar at the junkyard." I told them because it was hurting me.

Brady leaned far back in his seat and let his long, hard night wear off. "Yeah." Brady sighed after answering. "Some high school kid wrecked it." Brady didn't have to say anything else. He looked straight ahead. He was wearing cracked Danner boots made in Portland. His eyes were ringed with worry lines. A strained sadness hovered around them. He had a beard on his face. He wasn't the healthy, good-looking *Hot Rod Brady Robbins* who was still in love with Annie Kiss. He didn't chase after the beautiful girl who nobody really knew. He couldn't watch her luscious brown hair sway back and forth as she worked on her Cougar, or walked to work, or drove down Railroad Avenue with both her windows rolled down. He talked with his elbow propped up on the arm of his chair—a faint look of tortured happiness in his mud-colored eyes. He talked so we could all feel alive. He gestured with his cigarette and told a story with his eyes dreaming—his grubby clothes forgotten. He told us about being young and clean-cut. When everything was not simple or easy but still possible. He told us about how no matter how fast your car is, you can't drive away from some things. Because some troubles are harder and faster and uglier than you.

23

THE 1967 MERCURY

At first Brady's voice was cracked and broken. But as he went on it smoothed into the grooves of his story. His words flowed into a river of rain and blood and memory. He took us with him. His rambling traveled like spilled oil across a shop floor—steam escaping in hisses—the cracks in a radiator that scream. His stories lifted him—tormented. They left him broken and dreamless. Like a man serving a life sentence—he could only reminisce. The best times were over. The rest of his life was a perpetually unfulfilling joke. All he had were dull words—bleak and meaningless when compared with the real thing. His life. His girl. Even the cursed baby.

Brady said, "Annie worked at the ice-cream shop after school for two years straight to buy that car." His sentence was short and shaky but it meant so much. We knew how she walked to work every evening. Dished up thousands of ice-cream cones, slid milk shakes down the counter, made sundaes with cherries and whipped cream. She smiled automatically. She wiped her hands on bleached rags. She served uncomplainingly. Even when the customers were rude and demanding. Because there was no talking back. There was no defending. She could not leave her post. She had to keep smiling. She had to dish up ice cream. Her hands grew dry and red from the bleached rags.

The car was the only thing she ever owned. She rebuilt the 289 herself. Annie was damn proud. *Damn proud* of that car. She named the Cougar's paint job creamy pinky. It had gold flecks and four layers of clear coat. She insisted on that extra clear coat. She said she wanted her paint to look wavy. Like ice cream.

Annie could sit on her hair. It covered her back like a mantle. It crowned her thin body. She wore matching boots that went up to her knees, leather jackets that fit her curves, red lipstick, short skirts, blunt-cut bangs, and a teasing, all-knowing half smile. Her hair hung down her back and alongside her face. It matched her eyes. The color reflected in her pale pink skin. Her hair was a wall. It was untouchable and unnamable. It was hard to remember after it was gone. It put you under a crazy-drug spell. You couldn't recall why it was so beautiful. You couldn't put your finger on why you watched it so closely.

Annie was fifteen when I met her. She was wild and unstable. Annie was a fast girl. A head scrambler. A flirtatious manipulator. She was a hard-ass when it came to money. Tough as nails when it came to getting what she wanted. We got along just fine.

We hung out downtown at Kneeland Park. Kids dropped by to see us. We had chin-up contests on the monkey bars. We smoked cigarettes and drank Dr Pepper. I remember laughing.

One day, I told her I was going to find her cousin.

"Jimmy James?" she asked wisely.

I nodded, and told her I didn't believe in destiny. That night I left her at the park and walked uptown to the All Night Diner alone. Things happened quickly. All of a sudden Annie and I were sixteen and driving. I had a best friend, and we visited Jimmy James and Brady every weekend.

I'll never forget the day that trailer was stifling hot and smelled like sweaty feet and old food. We told the boys to make their own dinner. Drove to the river without them. Waved good-bye in cowboy boots and bikinis. Pretended not to hear them pleading with us to come along. Stifled giggles as they tried in vain to wave us down. We bought ourselves chocolate milk shakes at a roadside stand. We drove with all the windows down.

Brady fiddled with an alternator on the table. "She lived in that car," he said.

Fitz and I both nodded softly.

He went on, "Sometimes she sat in our driveway for hours listening to music and smoking her Camel Wides. I remember pulling up one day, and she didn't hear my engine, she had Reverend Horton Heat up real loud. She had her feet stuck out the window and her shoes kicked off. I seen her toes point and swing to the music. I just sat and watched her. It was sunny. She had this pink polish on her toes and the sun was shining across her legs. I suddenly wanted to hold her feet in my lap but I never knew when it was okay to touch her." Brady sighed and spit over the railing. It arced professionally. Not a drop fell on his front porch.

I knew Annie lived in her car because she had a mean daddy. I thought he was like that because she was so beautiful. His wife,

Annie and Stiv's mama, died when she was seven. He never got over it. He drank too much. Knocked them both around and then cried about it. Annie Kiss hated him. She hurried to get away. The hard part was that she loved her daddy just as much, if not more, than she hated him. Loved him more than I could understand, loved him more than I wanted to know.

He wasn't always like that. He wasn't like that before their mama died and they were just kids running around on the creek bottoms. Jimmy James told me so. He remembered Annie's mama hanging laundry in the backyard. He remembered when her daddy turned mean.

But to Annie, her daddy was her daddy. The only daddy she knew. The only daddy she ever had. No matter what he did to her, she still tried to make him happy. She *still* tried to help him get better.

Brady clenched his giant fists around the alternator without realizing it. He was clenching them so hard the blood drained out of them. His finger muscles strained and trembled. He shook from his anger and the feeling that it was too, too late. Fitz and I weren't really there for a moment. Brady's feelings took up all the energy on the porch. He struggled for a few seconds—to him it was a miserable eternity. He shook his head, shook it off. His *coulda beens* would follow him around his entire life. He went on doggedly, croaking at first, "Her daddy was pretty pissed when she stopped coming home. We saw him screaming and cussing at her when she walked out the door away from him. All of the sudden she was grown and he was an old man.

"And he saw us waiting with the engine running. And it was like he realized all at once that we could kill him. So he couldn't really do nothing but yell at her. And watch us outta the corner of his eye.

"He'd gotten worse as she got older. When Stiv stopped being around as much. Stiv got out as soon as he could. Bummed around from couch to couch. Soon as he was sixteen he got a job at the shipyard. So then Annie got all his anger. He was always mad at her. Talked to her like she was a dog or somethin'. The trailer they lived in had this mold growing up the side of it that never really got washed off. Whenever I see mold like that I get reminded of how hotheaded I felt when she left, and he called her those names. It wasn't true—none of the things he accused her of. It made me mad. I had to keep my mouth shut, though, if I wanted to be with her. Her daddy knew it, too. So I just stared at that mold and the yard around it. I have it memorized. Her daddy's old International rotted in one corner, her pile o' shit brother's broken-down Tempo was in the middle. Two Chrysler minivans and a Charger that coulda been nice if he'da done something with it. I can see the entire piece of property when I shut my eyes. She was standing out there in her jacket getting rained on because they didn't have such a thing as a porch—just a doorway outside and slippery wooden steps. She always seemed so thin and bowed-in when he did that, when he got real deep into her. She just took it. Shrunk down into herself, her legs shook, and her face got white so her lips stood out. The blood seemed to drain right out of her body. But her *hair*." Brady shook his head in amazement. "It stayed so *alive* and brown.

"She snapped out of it by the time she got to the car where we were all waiting for her—me and Jimmy James and this geeky kid named Carrot who lived around there. Stiv wasn't there. He prolly woulda brawled with his old man. He was always doin' that. I hope we were good for her. A *whole car* filled with real friends huddled against each other smoking cigarettes in the rain with the engine running and the radio on. A *whole car* filled with guys who would've done *anything* for her. We knew her daddy was mean and full of shit and told her so when she finally put her suitcase in the trunk and got in for the last time. She shook her head like she wanted us to bug off." Brady picked up the alternator and slammed it back down on the table. "I never wanted nobody else my whole goddamn life." He was shaking.

He'd been thinking about it every day. He pieced all the words together perfectly. He tried to sort it out and still came back to the same thing: the feeling of standing at the edge of a huge crevice in the earth—a loaded gun in his hand.

"We'd run away together before that. During the summer mostly. We camped out in the woods with sleeping bags and tarps. We built fires every night, and I stole beer from my ma. We'd move around so's nobody could find us. That was when we were younger. She bought that car so she could sleep in it when she needed to. And she did. Quite a bit. Way more often than she let on to any of us. It had a big-enough trunk to keep a box of clothes and all that. She felt more at home there than anywhere. I can't stop picturing her all alone sleeping on that bench seat in the middle of the woods. Pissing behind trees and brushing her teeth using a water bottle. She was tough, though. Wouldn't ever ask any of us for a goddamn thing. I got a job and moved to town along with Jimmy James, and I guess I kinda left her. She wanted out of her daddy's trailer for good, and she knew that to do it she needed cash. Fast. She wouldn't move in with me. She had this idea that she wanted to do everything herself.

"Soon enough, Jimmy James caught wind that she was selling weed. And her sleeping out there all alone waiting to get robbed. He was pissed from head to foot. Drove her over here fast to give her a talking-to. He was shaking all over. The only other time I saw him *that* mad was when I had too much to drink and wanted to go for a ride in my Galaxie. He put me in a headlock and stole my keys that time." Brady stared at his boots and thought.

Fitz and I let him talk. We let his words run out and connect to long, long silences. "She was the one I always thought would be able to get out. She stayed in school. She was always better than me—bigger than this town, too smart for a guy who don't even got his GED. I thought she would be on the top somewhere, giving orders in the tallest building, at the front of her field. All her teachers thought it, too, always took extra interest in her assignments, gave her the best grades, the most attention. I couldn't figure out why she would want to hang out with me except for the fact that Annie Kiss was as loyal as loyal could be.

"So when she ended up pregnant we were real mad. Because we knew who the father of her baby was. Because when she wasn't with us, she was alone in her car or locked up in that trailer with her daddy.

"And neither of *us* had ever touched her."

Brady stopped and took a drag of his fourth cigarette with a shaking hand. The alternator was back on the table. His heart was breaking, breaking. His eyes were wet. His voice far away. "She didn't try to hide it like some girls would have. Didn't start wearing baggy sweatshirts all of the sudden. She just quit smoking cigarettes and was more careful about eating vegetables. No more Dr Pepper. She started walking. Finally moved all her stuff into my bedroom. Just like that. Suddenly she wanted me to hold her. Be with her all night. I tell you I was in heaven and hell at the exact same time. I had some money saved up, and I took her on the only vacation she ever had. Went camping on the Sol Duc for a whole week. She didn't stop smiling—not even in her sleep. We were so happy. That's where those rocks come from." He nodded toward the pile that was still stained with red.

The Sol Duc River was Brady's promised land. He loved those banks and that water more than he could ever say.

"She was excited about it. She made it seem like a natural thing—to be carrying a baby like that. Usually girls got kicked out of high school for getting knocked up. But for once the school minded its business. She was real close to graduating. I tried to talk some sense into her. I wanted to marry her and raise her baby like it was mine. And I would have, too, would have loved her the whole rest of our lives and that baby, too. Would have loved every minute of it. Jimmy James told her to lie on the birth certificate and say that the baby was mine. We knew that turning her daddy in was out of the question. This town is too small. The newspaper would have printed it. People would have remembered forever. But they wouldn't remember me and her having a shotgun wedding and a baby too young. We would have been just like everyone else.

"She left one morning and didn't show up at school. When it got dark I started worrying, and we looked for her. Joey—and you, Fitz—and Jimmy James stood with me at the end of the driveway of her daddy's house trying to see inside of that trailer.

Her car was there but we couldn't see her. We threw sticks and rocks at her bedroom window. I didn't want her daddy to hear us and get mad and hurt her. We thought she might be locked inside. He'd done that before—locked her in her room. Finally, we went in there with baseball bats and chains and everything. We broke the door down and looked all through that place. Didn't find nothin'—no clue as to what went on there. Nothing 'cept . . ." Brady's shoulders trembled just a little bit. So slightly it was heartbreaking.

Fitz tilted his head to the right and helped Brady with his story. "Nothing 'cept that big ol' bloodstain. And that little hole dug in the backyard."

Brady put his head in his hands and stared at the floor. I pictured the boys standing around her Mercury under the wet fir trees outside the fence in the front yard. Looking devastated. Watching the sunrise over the whole sorry place. Golden light glinting off broken-down minivans. The Charger. The yellow grass. Standing there and none of them saying a goddamn word. Waiting. Knowing it was too late.

It was five days before I found out she was stripping in Bremerton. Dancing topless for money under the overpass. I went there alone. The doorman wouldn't let me in. Said I was too young. I told him my best friend was in there. That I needed to talk to her. I pictured her covered in bruises. Belly skin sagging. The men watching her dull-eyed and stoned. Giving her money. Watching that pretty golden-brown hair. Lost in their dreamworlds. The bouncer said tough luck. Asked when I would be eighteen. Said they were always looking for dancers. I glared at him. He said he would tell her I was here, and she could meet me out back. I said *fine*. I knew he was lying. He would let me wait there until I gave up. He knew that some people's resolve dissipates with time. He didn't know that mine boils over. I threw my cigarette on the pavement. Ground it into dust underneath my heel. When I called the Man from Angel Road I was already shaking. Anxiety pulled me from reality in long strides. I was floating somewhere high above the highway. Above Sinclair Inlet. The brackish water of a hazardous-waste site. The suspended organisms dying off in great numbers.

The boys showed up with a whole crew in three cars. Took the bouncer by surprise.

Annie was up there—the newest dancer. Brady talked her down from the stage as Fitz danced to the music himself and told the men to keep their dicks in their pockets.

"Nothing to see here, folks." Joey waved his hands in front of Annie and Brady. The small strip club was suddenly swarming with bald, laughing teenaged boys eager for violence. Erections melted into shrinking testicles. Fitz propped the door open to let the sunlight in. Blue cigarette smoke found the sky and rose joyfully. The owner stormed out from the back room. Said he was gonna call the cops. Jimmy James stood before him. Got so close their chests touched.

"Please do," he said as he looked down on the older man. "Because you should be ashamed of yourself." Annie was underage, and he could prove it. He waved her driver's license in front of the man's eyes. It wasn't long before the security guards mobbed them.

They wouldn't have done that if they had known how much the Man from Angel Road loved to fight. That he perhaps loved it more than he should. That he was always up for a brawl. And would not back down. He was the last one standing every time. Jimmy James's father beat the living shit out of him regularly until the day he realized his firstborn son was grown, and left. Nadine's bruises finally healed. And Jimmy James worked like a dog ever since. His body had not forgotten these things.

At the strip club underneath the overpass, ashtrays flew through the air. Serving girls screamed. Annie beat a sailor off Brady's back with a chair. The wood cracked and splintered. The black vinyl tore. The older men cringed. They scowled and walked to their cars. Annie finally made everyone stop. Standing there in her underwear. Seething.

She got dressed and followed them out the door, and we all left. She rode home in the front seat of Brady's Galaxie with dead eyes. She had a coke habit and a chip on her shoulder. The next morning she sold her car and went straight back up Highway 3. Nobody heard a word from her for a month.

Then she called Brady, and he picked her up again. He told her he knew the whole story about who the daddy of her baby was and what happened. Wouldn't blame her one bit or judge her if she would just clean up and start walking a straight line.

"She didn't have much to say," he said. "I wasn't even sure what part of her was left. She'd moved on to heroin. I s'pose that stuff can eat up a girl pretty quick." Brady tended Annie. She threw up in their bedroom. He went through days of hell: *she screaming and he watching her body shake.* He went through all that just to watch her walk away and shoot up again. *Damn.*

"I still would have married her," he said. "She still had that strut—that *hair.* Funny how someone can be so beautiful and totally fucked up at the same time. But she was real depressed and left again. I let her go. *You deserve someone better* was the last thing she ever said to me. I had my job to think about. Thought maybe tough love would cure her. Heard bits and pieces of her here and there. I didn't know what to do. Life moved on for everyone but me. I couldn't keep driving around the country chasing after her when she was determined to destroy herself anyway. I thought she'd come back for good when she was ready. So, I just kept working. And Joey went to Alaska. And Fitz, you got that job at the gas station. I still thought about Annie, kept thinking I'd see glimpses of her everywhere. I drove to Bremerton at night when I couldn't sleep. I looked around those neighborhoods and watched for her.

"Everyone stopped bringing her up whenever they saw me. The answers to everyone's questions were written all over my face."

He picked up the alternator again. "She didn't leave nothing here but a journal with two photos stuck in it. A picture of her daddy, and that photograph you took of her sitting on the hood of that Mercury Cougar the day she bought it. All us boys standing around her and grinning. Haven't had the heart to read her words yet. Guess I'm a little afraid of what's in there."

Brady Robbins stopped talking. All the life went out of him. His free arm lay like spaghetti at his side. His face was blank. His cigarette had burned out a long time ago. The sour smell of it wafted up with the wind. It blew raindrops on us. I drank another beer. Brady's worry lines crawled toward his hairline. I tried not to let the guilt eat at me. But I kept feeling like I did something wrong—like I deserved to be sitting there staring at the reddish-black rocks. I slid three of Fitz's cigarettes out of his pack, lit them one by one, and handed two over. Our shoulders stooped forward in a line. I studied our misery—became a student of it and the exhaled smoke.

I thought of lost chances. My life stretched before me—empty. Jimmy James burned up in the fire of his own anger. An easy target. A loaded pistol that backfired. Strong and weak. Dangerously brilliant and fatally alive. I looked at Brady. We hadn't saved our lovers from themselves. We should have held on for dear life. Dropped everything. Died trying.

I kept Annie's secrets for her. I kept them long after the stretched summer night she spilled them to me in the dark of Brady's living room—after the boys went to sleep. When she was still pregnant with her baby. The day that Kat came. After Jimmy James made Kat so angry she became a person. When I drank the rest of my bottle of wine and talked lowly with my best friend. Annie told me about her daddy.

"He doesn't mean it," she said. "He's usually so drunk I don't think he remembers. He misses my mom so much . . . it makes him crazy." After a moment her eyes creased happily at the edges. "But Brady loves me anyway."

Her lips were softly pursed—her eyebrows made diagonal lines across her forehead that pointed toward her nose. She bloomed with love and motherhood. She was ready to let the past be the past. She was strong. I was glad. She smoothed the quilt lying over her knees. She'd been straightening pictures and folding things. The living room behind us was neat and tidy. There were potted flowers in the windowsill. Herbs grew from small terra-cotta planters in special corners that received sunlight. The kitchen didn't smell so much like deep-fried things since she moved in.

She told me she was going to her daddy's place to lay it all down in the morning. She was going to tell him her plans. Say that she was marrying Brady Robbins—raising her baby with him. She felt she needed to say this to her daddy so he would know. And that that's why she left.

Fitz didn't ride along with Brady as he took me back to Cota Street. Brady looked through the windshield steadily. His old laugh lines showed up in the early pink light. He parked in front of my dad's house and held on to the steering wheel with closed eyes. His body was suddenly foreign—it belonged to a stranger. He was morbid and bitter and worn. He was suddenly a terrifying man with weaknesses and vulnerabilities and things he could not control. I clenched the awful seat. That's when I knew: There is a certain peace when the blood dries and hardens. And scar tissue in knuckles builds in circles, swelling. Skin always grows back when the violence is over. You have only yellow bruises and a metallic reminder in your teeth. You will never be the same. Brady was weak and rambling as his wounds healed. His shaved head bowed as he told me, "They'll take it all away." We watched the work-release truck on Cota Street flash red with swaying tools. I stepped down to the curb and slammed the door. I kicked the speckled pavement as bodies in orange suits pressed desperate against the bars.

I stood there and watched the prisoners and the cold sun. Brady drove away. My brain was ground hamburger meat. I leaned against my truck in the driveway—it was a cold cement wall. My anger gathered like bubbles rising.

I didn't sleep that day. I cleaned the house on Cota Street. Colin followed me from room to room. I told him, instead of Brady, about Annie's notebook. How it had disappeared and then shown up again. How Annie had noticed it missing just as I swallowed my last drop of wine the day before she went to her daddy's trailer. Colin scratched the back of his neck. "Annie still got that Mercury?" he asked.

I tossed and turned in my bed that night. I woke up wanting something I wasn't sure of. My arms and legs slid through cold sheets. I flailed in frosty seawater. Annie wrote poems on the banks of the Sol Duc. River rocks glistened with water that was alive. My arms searched my pillows. They reached for a man who wasn't there.

24

HONEY BURST

The Man from Angel Road came home early from Bremerton. He told me what happened—was glad I was awake when he got there—thankful for my warm body to hold on to. He turned the stereo up while he showered, brushed his teeth. I listened to his bathroom noises and fell back asleep.

He woke me with his clean mouth. Led Zeppelin floated to us over the earth-toned throw rugs in front of the record player. I curled into his body. I had it memorized. We fit together perfectly. Our skin touched, our hearts beat, our lips and hands couldn't stop. We searched each other quietly, asking and saying: *Are you still you? I miss this.* We moved against one another—clothing, sheets, distractions fell to the side. We rose above it all. A vanilla candle burned. We were alive: *muscular, naked, sweaty, young.* We found the strings that held us together. Our worries waited—the rent was still late—the electric bill too high. But we didn't think about any of it.

I hovered over his body. I listened to him breathe. I felt his body tense and then soften and then become mine. All mine. His boots lay in a tumbled heap at the door. A shaved head was pressed against the pillowcase. There were faded orange flowers printed on the secondhand cloth. The bright pallor of his skin made all other colors vague and muted. I missed him even as he was pressed against me—kissing my earlobe. I watched his chest. Where his heart beat so sincerely. I loved his nose, his fingers, the space where his neck met his shoulder blades. He began where I left off. He set one foot in front of the other. He walked beside me.

It hurt for some reason—was too simple and beautiful to last. Our path was painful. My heart expanded. And then exploded. This moment was only temporary. Everything would fade fast. I wondered what I would do when he was gone. When I had only my memories: *clean skin, musky scents, and firm calloused hands.*

Afterward, we lay still and spoke little. He sensed my thoughts. Turned onto his back and strummed his guitar—waiting for me. I finally kissed his kneecaps. He put his Les Paul down. There was a smile on his face that did not show teeth. He opened his arms, and I came to meet him. I spread myself over his skin and flesh and bones and beating heart. His body was wider and longer than mine. His arms squeezed the breath out of me. I knew for sure he was really there. He held on for that extra moment that meant everything. He didn't want to be anywhere but holding me. There was no hurry in his touch. I rested my cheek on his chest. Breathed into his tattoos. Timothy slept in his big-boy bed in the bedroom. Jimmy James checked on him. Left the bedroom door open a crack. I closed my eyes. The Man from Angel Road came back and crawled under the covers. I felt his breathing deepen into the heavy drone of final rest. I drifted off.

But my sleep was not silent—it wavered in and out of different worlds. A scream bubbled up from a rotten abyss—a scream that never reached my mouth, that stayed growling in my throat. I dreamed of grass blades, earthy brown gelatin, and shame. I woke up lonely. I felt Jimmy James leaving me. He would more and more often be *the Man from Angel Road*. Something was horrible and wrong. It would change us.

I watched him in the dark—his face relaxed and vulnerable. He was doomed by his anger, violence, and charisma. His beliefs he would never surrender. A heart that loved enough for all of us and more. But complicated, I knew. I wondered sadly what had gone wrong—what could possibly destroy the boy and the girl and the sleeping baby held together purely by spirit and love. I washed myself quietly in wavery candlelight. I left a note for him that said I would be back—that explained nothing. My sketchbook nestled under my arm. My drawing pencils fit snuggly in my pocket. I blew out the candle and walked to the All Night Diner. I drank coffee and thought. I sat in a booth alone. I tried to sketch the salt and pepper shakers. I stared at the rain soaking the black pavement of the parking lot. I watched the water gather into puddles. I watched it dribble onto the black rocks. I stared at the curb.

Three kids stole a bottle of ketchup from the struggling restaurant. They laughed outside in the rain. A boy with clean shoes tried to squirt the girls with ketchup. The plastic cap came off. The stolen ketchup plopped onto the ground. It missed the boy's shoes. It did not splatter on the girls' name-brand clothing. They screamed and got into their car. They all drove away laughing. The plastic bottle littered the parking lot. A minimum-wage worker picked it up and took it back inside.

I drew how the red ketchup looked on the black pavement—how the rain diluted it into thin, wavery red water. It turned the blacktop burgundy in the night.

When I glanced at my watch I gasped. I'd been gone for hours. I ran back down Cota Street as fast as I could. I was breathless when I rounded the curb. I looked down the alley. But it was the darkest part of night, and I couldn't see. I sensed movement and eyes on me—a fluttering of something outside our bedroom window. But when I came closer there was only the dumpster and a mangy alley cat who cowered. The carpeted stairs of the building were lumpy and cigarette-burned. The walls were a blur as I jumped the steps two at a time with adrenaline pumping through me. I burst into the apartment and saw Jimmy James sleeping safely. I hunched with my back to the door and began quietly sobbing. I felt sure I was going crazy. Jimmy James, who had never seen my tears, jumped up in terror. He instinctively pulled his boots on. The sound of broken glass filled the room. On the floor was a plain, black rock among the broken shards of glass. A cold wind gushed through the hole. Raindrops splattered the windowsill.

Timothy screamed.

I pulled the toddler to my chest in the dark of the bedroom and whispered to him. I shut the door.

"Fuck this neighborhood!" Jimmy James shouted from the

windowsill. "Fuck all of you!" He threw the window open in frustration and crawled out onto the fire escape in his boxer shorts. The glass cut his hands, and he bled. He looked down into the alley and slid down the ladder. He cursed all the way to the street but found no one. Whoever threw the rock was fast and wily—slinky and evasive.

He was shaking from head to foot when he finally came back up the front steps of the building. Too angry to calm down. Timothy had gone back to sleep easily. Jimmy James wanted to drive to Brady's right that second.

That's when I pulled him to me and begged him not to go. I reminded him that nobody was there but Annie. Just this once, I wanted him to stay with me in our twin bed. That's when he remembered I'd been crying. The rock stayed on the carpet while he kissed my hair and asked me questions. But I couldn't answer. It took a long time. His blood dried on my neck. I fell into an exhausted sleep.

But the Man from Angel Road remained unnerved. He knelt to pick up the rock while I tangled in the sheets. He examined it more closely. His fingertips were immediately smudged with dark red—wet with human blood less fresh than his own. He shrugged and threw it back out the window. He taped a blanket over the hole to stop the breeze.

25

GAS STATION BODY

Kat hid in the bushes and watched Jimmy James get in his truck and leave the little red car. She went in the back door of the trailer. She called Duane at the tattoo shop downtown where she knew he'd be. He jogged down Preacher's Slough Road in his ragged combat boots. His mind picked up a radio station all its own. The voices buzzed and competed with each other. It had been three weeks since he'd slept. He went through Brady's open back door. He didn't show his front teeth to Kat because they were brown rotten spikes. Kat and Duane smoked meth in the living room. Joey was still in Alaska. Fitz was at work at the gas station. Joey had sent Brady his rent money along with a letter to us all that said he'd made good money but the girl selection left much to be desired. The envelope with the letter and money was sitting on the kitchen table. Kat took the bills and stuffed them into her pocket. Duane and Kat lit candles. Annie didn't move from Brady's bedroom. She was a lump under the covers and an occasional low moan.

Duane was hoping for something later. He was hoping to revisit Kat's gas station body—and maybe explore Annie's, too. He thought of Kat's flesh that was always open—that took credit cards. He hadn't seen her in a long time. The meth made him stiff. His mind raced with thoughts of Kat's glazed eyeliner eyes. Her cigarettes. Her red-brown pubic hair. The fact that Annie Kiss was so woozy and unprotected.

Kat told Duane everything he'd been waiting to hear. She told him who she'd seen Jimmy James with in Bremerton, where they lived, and how they had to be stopped. They smoked more meth. Duane was very much alone aside from Kat. And being alone scared him. Even if Stiv hadn't gone to prison, he wouldn't have hung around much longer. Duane thought about the Man from Angel Road. How he had the nerve to walk upright. The fourteen-eye ox-blood boots. Duane had a bag of marijuana and he pushed it across the table toward Kat. She found a pipe in her purse. They got high quickly—as if they had no future. They drank all Brady's beer and Fitz's Jack Daniel's. The alcohol affected them little.

"We have to *clean*!" Kat told Duane suddenly. She threw Brady's leather gloves at Duane. She put rubber gloves on her own hands. He didn't understand but obeyed her by sliding on the leather gloves. They cut up pieces of the carpet to tape onto the edges of the table. They rearranged the furniture so that all the chairs faced east. They straightened every picture with a level. They talked and talked and didn't listen.

Finally, Kat stopped amid her preparations. Everything kept glaring at her—nagging.

She couldn't forget her original plan. She tried to concentrate. She lay down desperately with her face on the mutilated carpet. "Get the money!" she yelled helplessly at Duane. She beat her fists against the wall. They were running out of time. Her words dribbled out like the drool after vomit. "We'll need all the money!" Duane didn't understand. She was thinking of Mexico.

Kat's eyes were dry and red. She was losing it. She went into Brady's bedroom and pawed through his nightstand drawer. Duane followed and thought angrily about Jimmy James. How Kat was the one thing he had that Jimmy James didn't. Duane pulled Kat to him and squeezed her body. He smelled her cheap perfume. Her cigarettes. He leered at Annie in the bed and squeezed Kat harder. When he dug his pelvis into her she clawed at his face with her nails. "What are you? *Stupid?!*" She spit on him and kneed him in the stomach. It knocked the wind out of him, and he crumbled. After a few seconds he rolled over and stared at the ceiling. Kat found all the money from Brady's bedroom drawer and shoved it into her pocket.

Duane wanted to be somewhere else. He wanted to feel good and in control. He reached weakly for Kat's leg. He finally remembered the cabin by the lake, the happy little wife, the stream where he caught fish. "Will you marry me?" he asked Kat with his whole soul ready.

"No!" Kat screamed at him in exasperation and kicked his skull. He curled up again. This time in real anguish.

It was the first time she had ever told a man no, and it felt strange. The word cut out everything else in Duane's mind. It made him want her even more. He sat up dizzily. "I'll build you a cabin," he started out, and the words drifted off. He really wanted Kat to see what he was seeing.

Kat lifted the mattress and inhaled excitedly. "It's here!" she shouted with her bright yellow gloves on.

Annie sensed the movement and tried to sit up. "What the fuck is going on?" she whispered hoarsely.

Kat showed Duane the .45—the 1911 with the pearl pistol grip. Duane got angry. He was no fool. His mind swirled around the smell of peat mulch and marijuana seedlings. He didn't want to remember.

He thought instead of Kat's swastika tattoo, her glazed eyeliner eyes, her cigarettes, and her red-brown pubic hair. Her dirty gas station body. She was like an animal. He had to hold her captive underneath him—hold her so that she couldn't move—so she would never go away again. He had to teach her a lesson about stealing. He looked at the gun angrily.

That's when Annie gave a terrible fight. A fight that knocked down my paintings and tore holes in their flesh. Bite marks and screaming. Two black eyes on Kat's face. A sore scrotum for Duane. She got as far as the dirt lawn before the front porch. Where she and I had arranged those black rocks.

Kat finally held her down, and Annie's teeth were broken. A two-by-four lay discarded. Blood gurgled into the rocks through a broken jaw. Annie was no longer conscious. Kat talked quickly while she had the chance. It had to be Duane who pulled the trigger because she wanted to watch. They didn't have much time. It would make her want him—to see him do that. Kat lit up her crack pipe again. Duane's thoughts pulsed with sounds and colors and whispers. Annie lay close to death.

"They'll never know the truth," Kat told him assuredly. It was getting late.

Annie didn't move. She was still and cold then hot and shaking on the hard-packed earth. She moaned softly—a mountain of strength. Duane looked down at the gun in his hands. It was a pretty revolver. He thought the explosion would redeem him—make him worthy. He thought the blast would release him, clean away all the debris and confusing feelings—the voices. He pictured himself as the king of Cota Street—everyone finally giving him the respect he wanted. With Kat as his queen.

Annie's last moments were subdued, sick, and sleepy. She was already drifting away with the smell of burnt methamphetamines.

Kat slipped her hand in Duane's pants. Her fingers struggled blindly. She felt him there and smiled coyly. She went back into the trailer with an axe and hacked at the lockbox bolted underneath Brady and Annie's bed. She came back to stand beside Duane still holding the loaded gun.

"I have to, don't I, Kat?" he squeaked, and she nodded.

The blast did nothing that Duane had imagined. Instead of wiping clean all the curses, memories, and bright images, it pushed them closer to him until they all screamed at once. He gasped in terror at the sight of Annie's terribly mutilated body. He started shaking. The blood drained out of him. He wanted to distance himself from the dead girl and the live one. He looked up at the white trailer, and wished it was his. That he had good friends like Brady Robbins. Duane's knees were weak. His flesh dried up and disappeared beneath him. He sat down. In a puddle of his own regrets. They fell out of his head—scurried around his feet. Faster and faster. They chased one another. Until he could see nothing else—just a whirlwind of hopeless thoughts. And then everything stopped. And the silence jarred him. All he could think about was how he hadn't really meant any of it. But it was too late.

Kat shivered in the cold wind that blew. She watched the snot and tears drip off Duane's red and swollen face. He suddenly looked very young. The warm saltwater wet the rocks—made them obsidian. Duane dropped the gun and started jogging.

Kat bent down and scooped up a Sol Duc River rock and the .45. She ran after Duane—picked her way carefully through the dark clear-cut. They went back to the tattoo shop. Kat ran recklessly down Cota Street. She came back without the bloody rock. Duane woke someone and paid them to borrow their vehicle. They drove all the way up into the hills in a minivan. He threw the gloves out the window somewhere along the way.

Duane parked at his mama's trailer. There was no electricity again. He avoided his family and went straight to the fields his father once farmed. Kat followed him guardedly past the shootin' car. They were in the woods now. Deep in a place Duane knew well. They crossed a stream that trickled over shiny rocks. A barred owl hooted. Kat had never seen Duane so serene. He had sex with her absentmindedly and walked away. She scurried to put her clothes on and run after him. He had taken the gun.

Duane crawled over a stump pile covered in blackberry vines. Kat had trouble following him. She called for him to wait but he didn't listen. Her foot was stuck between two roots. She twisted her ankle and scratched herself on the vines. She felt herself being left behind by the only human being who had ever cared whether she lived or died. "Duane!" she was getting scared now. The meth was wearing off some.

She thought about his marriage proposal and her stupid reply. She was sorry. She began crying for the first time since she was eleven. Big, built-up sobs. Earth-shattering, body-breaking tears. She had trouble gulping air. She hid her face in her elbow. She finally thought of her mother. Her whole body convulsed. She choked on her emotions and yanked at her leg. She cursed her tattoos. She didn't know what they meant. Or why she had done anything that she had done.

Kat looked to where Duane had gone and saw a square of cleared land. He was standing in the middle on the freshly harvested earth. It was brighter there where the moon found him. With all her strength she parted the roots and slid her foot out. Her leg was gouged and bleeding.

Duane looked up at her. Even though she didn't want to, she met his inharmonious gaze. He looked right at her. Locked straight into her pupils. With the gun raised to his head. She saw him close his eyes first. Heard the gunshot second.

Duane's mama sensed the echo but closed her mind to it. She sighed in relief when she heard the minivan start up and leave. She rose to make her biscuits shakily in the early morning darkness.

At the first gray of dawn, she covered her hair with a navy blue scarf. She walked down to the marijuana field and found her son. She'd been expecting this. Or something close to it. She thought carefully of the television crews. And the reporters with notepads. And the months of work she'd put into those fields.

She picked a spot south—underneath a massive cedar that fell and was rotting. She buried him there. With a love nobody else knew. She prayed over his body. She buried him deep.

26

MEAT FOR NADINE

The morning was cool and steamy before they found Annie. After Brady came home.

Before they arrested Jimmy James.

I huddled against a tree in the Skokomish unit—bare arms to my ragged chest—the boredom biting into me. I'd been leaning against the tree for quite some time. Hours. Since sunrise. Not as patient as Jimmy James. Something was wrong. The waiting piled up. I bit my lip. I wanted to sit, but when I was sitting I wanted to stand. I was making too much noise. Although I had slept, I had not rested. That morning I had washed myself in scent-blocking soap, my clothes in odorless detergent. I was trying not to stare at Jimmy James's back, in order to give him privacy. He knew when I was looking even if he couldn't see me. I saw chanterelles growing under some Doug fir. I would remind Jimmy James to stop there on the way back.

The herd came all at once. They appeared from behind trees and evaporated into bushes.

They floated down from the sky—their stinky, animal odor filled up my nostrils all at once. Their cries surrounded us.

I watched the arrow leave the camouflaged hunting bow—arcing high—a strong, loud absence of sound as it hit the animal's flesh. Behind the foreleg. A solid shot.

The large animal took a short time to die. We waited where we stood. We did not chase her. We watched the bushes where she disappeared in her death-run. We tracked her forty yards—followed traces of bright, bubbly lung blood and broken salal. Jimmy James's boots churned up no leaves or dirt out of a strong, hard-learned habit. The elk lay on the ground—a fat doe. *Doe meat is more tender*, he'd said that morning. Her once-heaving sides were still.

I watched him mouth a personal, silent prayer to some nameless and cruel god. He gutted the animal with respectful hands—dove deep into the cavity of the body. He threw the truck keys to me and told me to go get his brothers. I left him while he finished. He would need all of us to help drag the animal to our truck. I stopped before I entered the thick tree line and turned around. I watched him on the grass alone with the elk carcass. I worried for him. I thought of cougars—their large, slinky bodies and silent paws. He worked methodically and easily. His arms were crimson. The blood turned dark as the air hit it. His bald head bowed for a moment. The steam rose up around him. He stayed there—motionless. I wondered if he was thinking of the meals we could have now. He looked so old sitting there. I had a sudden thought that I should turn around and go back to him—that I didn't have as much time as I once did. But I started moving again. I hurried away with my hands in my pockets. I drove to Angel Road.

I pulled up in the driveway and saw her. Nadine Blood: a Scorpio. As complicated as the prairie wind. Drastic and changing. Lofty and intimate—filled with hail and a hot, dry heat.

Nadine Blood: who asked little. Nadine Blood: who gave much. The first love of the Man from Angel Road. She lived in a brown single-wide with an ornate jungle garden climbing energetically around it. Her sons and Lupita lived with her. They helped her keep it up. There was much work to do—always. There was a small, shady pond and a whitewashed shed. Wet laundry hung by the woodstove to dry. Timothy was throwing rocks into the pond and squealing when the water splashed. "Gam!" he kept yelling excitedly at Nadine—wanting her to look. "Gam!" Pointing his chubby fingers.

I walked up behind him. Said his name softly so as not to scare him—didn't want him falling into the water. He turned and saw me. "Yee ah!" he yelled my name in a high-pitched voice. He spread his arms wide. I hugged him to my heart. I had bundled him in warm blankets early that morning. I had warmed up the truck before strapping him into his car seat. I held on to him for a moment just to smell him—feel him breathing—his black hair pressed against my nose.

I told him, "We can eat now." Nadine scowled. Her son shouldn't be out there alone. He should have taken his brothers instead of me.

Jimmy James took me because I'd wanted to learn. Nadine sensed the strange energy. She shook her head. She knew the problems of her firstborn ran deeper than hunting accidents. Nothing sat right. She stood with her pitchfork stuck in the soil—her elbow leaning on it—staring right through me.

Sagging grapevines hung heavily on a trellis. A split rail fence zigzagged around the apple, cherry, pear, and plum trees. Her porch held a spinning wheel and a kiln. There were bags of wool and clay. I saw her pottery wheel, pots she'd made and fired that were ready to sell.

She had a barn filled with home-brewed wine. Plum, dandelion, all the berries. The barn was where we kept our ammunition. The plan was always to meet here together when bad things happened. Her yard was an overwhelming regiment of pansies, sunflowers, and marigolds. We used her fresh thyme, parsley, basil, and rosemary to grill salmon. Pickled her peppers. Dried her lavender in bunches to use for tea and medicine. Made preserves out of her strawberries, blackberries, raspberries, salmonberries, and blackcaps. Dug up her potatoes to keep in the cellar under the barn. In the fall, we made pies from her pumpkins, froze and sautéed her yellow squash to eat with elk steak.

She planted the vegetables alongside herbs and flowers in a fragrant mishmash. Every plant was spotless, lush, and happy—planted in clusters. Corn, beans, and squash grew close together. The bean vines crawled up the tall corn stalks. The squash inched along the ground. Strong-smelling onions were planted around healthy carrots and cucumbers. There were spiders in the mounds of herbs. Marigolds grew unchecked. Cosmos, bee balm, and nasturtiums attracted swarms of happy bees in the springtime. Chives popped up everywhere. The butterflies pecked and fussed over the butterfly bush like little fairy nymphs.

Timothy was staying with her until Sunday. She liked to take him to town with her. She carried him proudly in her strong, bony arms. People couldn't walk by him without taking a second look and smiling—his face scrunched into one bright smile after another. His fat hands waved and reached. Nadine had helped at the birthing. Lupita had insisted.

Jimmy James and Lupita had a short affair: She was a nice girl. Her dress was periwinkle blue. She went with Jimmy James to the river. She bent her knees into the water—it rushed around her—she floated. The dress turned royal. She told him her mama felt better. That she was done being sick. The sundress was homemade—the ruffles hand sewn. Her hair was braided, and he was glad. The sun turned the river golden. The sun turned her hair red. She smiled like she had known him. She smiled as if they'd already made love. She was fourteen. Jimmy James a year older.

She attempted suicide after she gave birth. Ran Nadine's car off the road into a telephone pole even as her episiotomy stitches healed. She was examined by a psychiatrist—found to be an unfit mother. Jimmy James and I both knew—awful things had happened to her. Caused her young spirit to crumble. We couldn't blame her, really. She was so young. And Lupita had no legal guardian in the US after her mama died. And Timothy could not go back to El Salvador all alone. And Jimmy James held the screaming infant wrapped in a cheap, blue blanket to his chest. He could not say no. He was bound in an instant. Timothy grew darker as he got older. He didn't match us on the outside. His body curled between us as he slept. And fit perfectly.

Lupita went inside the brown trailer to wake Jimmy James's brothers. They pulled on blue jeans. They rubbed their eyes.

They ribbed me good-naturedly about waking them at noon. They poured cups of cheap, hot coffee from the pot. They drank it black. They shared a cigarette. They would help. They were sixteen-year-old twins. They followed me in Nadine's brown Buick after putting a bag of new potatoes in our truck. They fought about who would drive. The sun broke through the fog. We found Jimmy James easily. The blood already dried on his boots. I gathered my chanterelles. I carried the elk heart in a plastic bag. I walked behind the boys the five miles back to the truck. We heaved the body onto the bed. His brothers followed us. They hung the carcass from a hook in Nadine's backyard. The blood drained. Jimmy James was in a good mood. He fried bear sausage and potatoes for him and his brothers. Lupita and I ate toast and orange juice. Nadine stayed outside with Timothy. The brothers roughhoused. The twins fought against their elder. Jimmy James put them both in headlocks. He made them promise they would help process the meat the next day. *No matter what*, he told them, and released them from his grip. He glared and waited. Lupita stood halfway out of sight—behind the door. She nodded. The twins agreed, raised eyebrows at each other, and tried to be men about it. They sensed there were things they did not understand. They left to go fishing. Lupita curled up with Timothy on the hammock. She sang to him in a voice that was pure, and sad, and happy: "Someday I'll be good enough to ta-ake you home."

She was wearing a red dress. We went back to our apartment in town to shower and sleep.

The Man from Angel Road sat at the kitchen table with his chin on his fists—his elbows on the table. He looked younger— scared almost. His hands were rarely idle. The scar tissue in his knuckles throbbed. His stillness was a strange holiday. The sun shined in through the window. He'd missed me in the early morning—his body had searched for me in our bed and found nothing. He looked unabashedly into my face and read what was there. His eyebrows were like exclamation points. He leaned over the table and put his face close to mine. He didn't bat an eyelash. He put his hand on my arm. His palm pressed down. He pulled my chair close to him. I crawled into his lap and shivered. He put his arms around me, lifted my shirt, and pushed his forehead against my breasts.

I felt him all the way through, and it scared me. I held on. Nothing made noise for a while. Then we heard the train whistle blowing, and he carried me to our bed. We made sad love. I fell asleep in the early afternoon. He held me and waited.

27

PREACHER'S SLOUGH ROAD

Brady Robbins drove home from work. His body was tired but his heart floated elatedly.

He was thinking of Annie—knowing he'd probably stay up with her. He smiled anyway. He knew he'd been right to wait for her. He had a feeling this time it would be different. He stopped somewhere on his way home—spent his entire paycheck at the jewelry store. But the little black box held such promise. He would have to work more overtime. But now he would not worry about Annie. She would breathe next to him. He would sleep well. He drove with foggy eyes and smiled. His tires weaved lazily. He crossed the center line. No big deal. *Hot Rod Brady Robbins.* The name came to him—it sounded funny. He rolled the window down. He screamed *"Hallelujah!"* just for fun. An old lady getting yesterday's mail jumped at the sound of his voice.

He chuckled. He turned right on Preacher's Slough Road. He

drove for three miles. He pulled into his driveway. He jiggled his keys in his pocket. Nobody was perfect. He loved her anyway. He took three steps before his life would never be the same. The porch. The stairs. They jumped out strangely at him. He took three more steps before the bounce was gone from him forever. There. On the black rocks. Her brown hair down—wet and oddly alive-looking: *Annie.*

He sat down.

Annie.

He threw up.

Annie.

He decided it couldn't be real. He'd been working too hard. It was his awful mind playing awful tricks. He crumpled to the ground. He rested his cheek on the black rocks. There was an odd film over them. He stood. Then gave up and stumbled. He crawled. He grabbed Annie to him like he'd wanted to do for so long. He curled up on the ground with her. On the bloodstained black rocks. She did not respond to him. He stayed there. For as long as he could. His body numb. "*No no no,*" he whispered foolishly. His brain was not working right. "*No no no.*" Small protests. Massive breaths. The light rain let up.

Later, they took her away. They put her in a jaded, flashing vehicle. After physically removing him from her body. They tried to ask him questions. But he was not under arrest. He pushed through the crowd. Said *fuck off*—it was the only thing he could think of.

He stumbled blindly into his waiting Galaxie 500. The tires skidded across his yard. He drove, and he drove. Vague thoughts of going to Bremerton to find Annie assaulted him. The sun was rose red—it soon washed the streets in crimson. He turned left onto Binns Swiger Loop Road. He punched his dashboard and pressed down hard on the gas. Arcadia Avenue flew. His thoughts spun wildly. He was on the highway for only a moment. Then the dotted white line hypnotized him. The world spun stupidly. The sun stopped shining.

28

NAZI

That night they handcuffed Jimmy James before they kicked out his front teeth.

I sat up straight when I heard them outside. They'd been so quiet when they surrounded the apartment. Jimmy James opened the front door when he first heard them. He rushed out alone to the parking lot while I slept.

I was dreaming of Granny's property in the swamp. How the sun tried to burn off the fog in winter. How the sun always failed. When I woke, the dream fled from my reality—it didn't want to be part of it.

I was alone in bed. The door to the apartment was open. I got up and followed the sound of voices. The hallway was dark. There was no moon. Only the glow from the flickering streetlights lit my way.

As I took the steps in twos, I remembered Jimmy James telling me it was worse to fight a man who was scared than to fight a man who was bigger than you. A man who was scared was apt to do anything. Crazy things. If he was afraid, then adrenaline took over—the fight mode. He might bite and scratch and use scissors to stab you. Kick you in the groin. Stick your own switchblade in your back while you're doubled over. "It's better if he's not panicked," he'd said. "You're safer that way."

Outside the building, I saw how Jimmy James could be wrong. The police officers were not scared—they were cold and tunnel-visioned. They didn't do anything crazy. Jimmy James's young body jumped and rolled on the ground from the force of their blows. His eyes stared coldly ahead. He didn't shut them against the pain. He was watching for me through their legs—waiting. I listened to the dull thuds. They vibrated through the space of pavement that separated us. I ran, and my limbs felt stiff and sluggish. His eyes caught sight of me. A look of pure terror crossed his face. He had tried to avoid this.

I remembered how Jimmy James had also said, "The man in the fight who will surely lose is the one with the most at stake. If the girl he loves is there, it's over." He'd said it so many times. Now he told me to get into our truck. They kept kicking him. Their feet dove eagerly toward his ribs, his stomach, and the back of his head. One of them turned and saw me. He recognized my face.

"How you like your Nazi boyfriend now?" he asked. It stopped, and the cops watched me. They were teaching me a lesson. But I didn't learn. I had a dumb look on my face. Mouth open. Hands itching. There were too many things they did not understand. Their faces leered from across bare earth and black pavement. There were four of them.

I had a bloody, trampled feeling. Frustration brought angry

tears. I knew the rifle was in the hall closet. I knew the rifle was not an option. The Man from Angel Road had eyes that pleaded. There was nothing I could do. The uniforms of the police officers were clean. The parking lot was littered with trash. The dark sky glared. The empty space around me mourned.

Jimmy James writhed on the pavement. He told me again to lock myself in the truck. He said it through a bubbly mouth filled with blood. Bright red lung blood. He said it quietly. Forcefully. Coughed it: "*Get in the fucking truck.*" His words were exhausted and abstract—absent of emotion. His bottom teeth resembled broken bones poking out through the gaping, gigantic wound of his mouth. The lights on the squad cars were strangely dark. I tried to think of the colors they usually were: *Red. Blue.* I saw the blood dripping down the front of his black Guns N' Roses T-shirt. It turned the cotton burgundy—the color of dried blood on black rocks.

"Don't let them hurt you," he slurred so reasonably—pleaded with me. I couldn't resist his voice. The same voice that told me secrets—that talked so gently—assured Timothy it was okay when he scraped his knee. He sounded strained and tired. He kept all our memories away from him even as his blood turned black on the pavement.

The town cop smiled. He had short spiky hair and feet that sagged inward. He took a step toward me. I put my hand on the door handle of our truck. It was between them and me—unlocked. The other three watched him—breathing heavily. The town cop swelled with adrenaline. His eyes were bright with violence and entitlement. I quickly pulled the door open, climbed inside, and locked the doors. The cowardly movement plagued my nightmares for the rest of my life: *I left him there. On the cold pavement. His blood pooled on old, gray tar.*

I sat on the bench seat in shock. The cops went back to their business. I couldn't close my eyes at first. They were too dry. My face was haggard. I knew I would have been next. But mine would have been worse. It would have killed Jimmy James in a way that would never heal. They would have done it in front of him—in our apartment—with the pictures of our families watching—on the rug we picked out together—with our leftovers on the stove. My weak body would have failed me, and it would have killed him. He would rather feel the physical pain.

Because their blows were only temporary. The blood would dry and harden.

I wrenched my head away from the scene. Because later I wouldn't have been able to look him in the eye. He would have seen the pain hidden inside of me. The deep scar of me watching him. To see his body like a rag doll at their mercy. I rocked back and forth like a crazy person. I put my arms over my ears and squeezed my head. I shut my eyes. I put both feet on the horn of the old Ford. I pressed down hard. One long blast. Because I couldn't scream yet. Because I would keep my feet there until someone came.

I reached a place inside that felt watery and womblike—La Llorona beckoned me to join her on the riverbanks—the tears of blood dripped from her eyes onto the front of her white dress. There was mist and sad singing. I was drawn away by the sound of loud thumping on the top of the truck. Like dirt clods hitting metal.

Brady and Fitz were banging on the windshield and the ceiling of the cab. My feet flew off the horn. I knocked against

Brady's hard chest when I opened the door. It felt hollow as if his heart had fallen out.

The detective pulled up in a black Crown Victoria. The cops stopped what they were doing. There was an uneasy feeling among them. He slammed his door and gestured toward them angrily. "Are ya'll *crazy?*"

The town cop with crooked feet glared and said, "He's a fighter."

I watched my eighteen-year-old boyfriend stumbling like a drunk—his balanced, righteous walk turned into an old man's bar stagger. He fell. The cop with crooked feet pulled him to the car by his handcuffs. Cold mud gathered on his skin from the bare spots in the apartment lawn. His boxer shorts ripped and slid down his body. His unlaced boots pulled off his feet. I couldn't say the words that were boiling up inside of me. I choked instead.

Brady's face was the color of ash. His head was bandaged. His teeth were bloody. He'd left the hospital even as the nurses yelled at him to stay. He held me, and it felt strange. Because he needed me to support him. Because his arms circled and squeezed for dear life. He rested his head on the cold metal of the truck behind me. His Bronco was on the bare lawn—the Super Swampers dug into the mud. He was far away from everything. Suspended above the horrible scene.

Fitz looked like a lost boy with his hands in his pockets. Guilt showed plainly on his face. He looked at me, shrugged, and said, "I didn't know." He'd walked home to the mess of the silent ambulance, the paramedics, and police officers. The detective wanted to search his red Honda—had questioned him for three hours. But Fitz couldn't answer except to tell them, "I don't know. I don't know what happened."

Neither Brady nor Fitz could believe the words they told me: *Annie's dead.* They stood next to each other beside the truck. I stared at their boots. I ran to gather the fourteen-eye oxbloods from the blacktop.

The detective went back to his car. He wrote things down in a notepad. He gestured me to him. My body trembled under my thin T-shirt as I walked. He scratched his head and offered me his jacket. Finally he asked, "Were you with him last night?" And I couldn't answer. There was no voice left in me. My thoughts drifted over the All Night Diner. The waitress and the soccer kids. I realized I'd left Jimmy James twice. Twice when it really mattered.

The cops were laughing together for some reason. They watched me. The dull thud of the violence stayed in my brain. The reverberations left imprints. The bones broke over and over. I would never be the same. The world was only one color: *the color of life and death.*

"I know your boyfriend isn't a white supremacist," the detective was saying matter-of-factly. "But his political beliefs are a little extreme, aren't they?"

I didn't answer.

"I suppose he hasn't told you what he's been doing at night lately?"

I shook my head no. The detective nodded toward the cops. "Those Neanderthals don't really get it. But they're also sick of looking like assholes for not getting anything on him."

I wasn't sure why he was telling me these things. I felt very tired. He slipped me his card. I felt my body lose its shape.

"Can he afford a lawyer?" He looked at me.

Again, I didn't answer.

He sighed. "Well, he's been busy. Was he in Seattle yesterday?"

I shrugged.

"Well, I'm sure you've watched the news."

I smelled the detective's aftershave on his jacket. He had brown hair and kind eyes—the vaguest hint of a Mississippi accent. I stuffed his card in my back pocket.

He smiled sadly, and something clicked in my head. He spoke again lowly, "He's not so happy about the prison being built, is he?"

I looked at him, smiled bitterly, and thought, *Good cop.* I looked at the group of local police officers recounting their recent antics and thought, *Bad cop.* I gave the detective his jacket back. "Thanks." I said, "Really." I walked away.

That morning, Jimmy James's prints were lifted from the steering wheel of the Honda. The car held Annie's bloody rag and the tissue paper from Kat's pocket. The needle rolled back and forth on the floor. With Annie's blood all over it. Traces were found on our throw rug under the window among broken glass. And Jimmy James's own blood had dripped into the brown fiber.

In the alleyway on Cota Street, the detective confiscated the bloody rock. In a dumpster behind the All Night Diner, a sixteen-year-old employee discovered a fired-off 1911. There were fingerprinted bullet casings scattered across more black rocks from the Sol Duc. And in a trailer on Preacher's Slough Road, there was nothing left.

I picked up Jimmy James's teeth while the detective put the rock in an evidence bag.

Jimmy James bled and waited in the backseat of the cop car. I saw him slump forward in handcuffs and hit his head on the hard plastic. The police finally took him away. The detective poked around the building alone.

Brady leaned his back against our truck. He slid down the side and bumped his head against the steel. I heard the *thunk thunk* of his shot nerves. He huddled under the open truck door as if it would protect him. He put his forehead on his knees. His shoulders shook. He didn't see anything for a while.

I stared at the brown spots of decay on Jimmy James's incisors. His teeth looked useless and alone in my palm—even after I wiped the blood off them. The red stained my hands. It dried in the rims of my cuticles. I didn't wash it away.

I stuffed the teeth in my pocket and poked Fitz in the ribs. I told him we had to get out of there. He looked confused. I rifled through Brady's jacket pocket for his keys. Brady looked up in bewilderment. "Come *on*!" I was angry and frantic. I tried pulling him up myself but was helpless against his dead weight. "Brady!" I screamed in his face. I tried to break through his dull mask of grief and head injury. He winced and closed his eyes.

The detective stopped what he was doing and assessed the situation calmly. I knew more policemen would come. There might be television cameras and microphones. Reporters and tape recorders.

"We have to *go*!" I jabbed Brady urgently. There was a block of ice in my chest that was melting. Each drop of cold water made my stomach clench in shock. Brady stumbled to his feet and leaned dizzily on Fitz. They trudged slowly to the Bronco. I jumped in and revved the engine.

There was only one place left to go. The O'Neel swampland waited.

29

JUNE IN ST. LOUIS

It was June in St. Louis. I listened to the Cracker song about cigarettes and carrot juice on my Walkman at the laundromat. It was warm and Sunday. I watched the television that was bolted to the wall. A stranger helped me fold my sheets. The news show talked of "drugstore cowboys." I felt a chill crawl up from my belly and into my heart.

I bought a vanilla-and-sandalwood-scented candle at a discount store while my jeans finished drying. I bought crayons and paper. Acrylic and watercolor paints. I checked my pants. They were still damp.

There was a deep unrest in the wind that flitted in and out of the brick buildings. I watched a line of children dancing in the parking lot. The scattered trash that rabid dogs gnawed to pieces blew in front of them. The arms of the children sliced through the sky. Their feet cut jagged wedges into the humid, whipping breeze.

They were bright and alive. My own arms and legs felt leaden and dead. I was standing on a piece of pavement that spun wildly.

The phone was shut off at Dad's house. He hadn't paid his bill. I listened to the recording. The computer voice left me stranded at the pay phone on a street corner.

I set the vanilla and sandalwood–scented candle on the cardboard box beside my camping mat when I got home. I opened my window. I lit the wick with a long, wooden match. I lay down on my mattress. I waited for the warm scent of vanilla and sandalwood to float over me. I looked at my library book about Robert Johnson. I thought about a rock tumbling down a hillside. A ball of fire that kept feeding. A sphere of hard-packed snow that rolled and gathered speed. It was hot and humid in Mississippi where Robert Johnson was born. I understood why he had so many women. The obsessive compulsiveness of new love. Trying to erase the aching pressure. I closed my eyes. The sun went down. I watched the empty eyes of Shenendoah next door grow dark. I listened to Mazzy Star with the lights off. I could not get comfortable. I was a forgotten dishrag in a washing machine— drenched in harsh detergents and spun until I was formless—icy and wrung out and waiting.

The memories—they would not leave: Jimmy James's Honeyburst Les Paul. His hands on our old Ford truck. How his back was always straight. Eyes that were sad and diplomatic. Fighting a losing battle. The terribly large burden.

I moved through my apartment shuffling inside of the fourteen-eye oxblood boots. I folded everything. Scrubbed away my pencil drawings on the walls, put my clothing away in boxes, and gave my food to the few neighbors who remained.

In the morning, I went to work early with the extra paper and crayons and paint. I sat and recorded everything I saw at Meadows. I marked and measured colors and faces and all the shades of gray. Mrs. Halls corrected papers at her desk in the early morning light. She let me sit quietly and watch her at 7 a.m. The end of the school year loomed. My pencil moved assertively. She forgot about me—marked the children's notebook paper with a red pen. She scowled, rubbed her temples. Wanted her children to be prepared for a hard life. Tried to push away the dreadful stress.

My eyes burned at my small table. I finished and started another drawing without thinking. My pencil revealed a hand covered in chicken blood reaching out of murky water. It was a flag of surrender. It pleaded for help.

I hung my head and choked on the smell of cut grass and burnt gunpowder. I stumbled out of the child-size desk. There was no more air. I kept thinking: *Mima is coming with us.*

Mrs. Halls's long arms were around me. She held on as I fought for breath. She tried to comfort me. But I was beyond logic. I told her I had to go home. Even as I said the words, my childhood turned stormy and disappeared in a hail of buckshot.

30

SWAMP WATER

Colin was thinking about the smell of grass from Mima's soccer cleats, thinking that maybe she'd been right to go. That David was a dark place. There were no streetlights. The new prison was built on land that had been clear-cut. And replanted. And clear-cut again. There were miles and miles of swamp and alder. And hungry cement walls.

David officials attempted to renovate downtown. They waited for the tourist money. There would be sculptures, a little museum, and antique stores that sold costume jewelry. Colin wanted to leave but he knew there wasn't anywhere safe. The land pulled and pulled at him. The rich men in suits and uniforms wanted him out. The Cota kids were not part of their plans. The men wearing city shoes did their best.

Colin and Ratboy ran into Carrot, who was buying a tall can of malt liquor at the deli. Carrot, who had been around for a while. Carrot, who was tall and skinny with red hair. Who had stooped shoulders and a cowboy hat. Who still lived with his bad-tempered mother. Colin asked Carrot what he was up to. Carrot told them he was picking up painkillers from the pharmacy for his mother, and the tall can was for *her*. Colin remembered his mother as the cook at the grade school. How she had a mustache and a lip full of chew. Colin said he had a dollar, and Ratboy had seventy-three cents. He said that Carrot should buy them another tall can with the money and then come over and drink with them. Carrot wasn't sure. He was supposed to go right home. But he didn't have very many friends. And Colin was good-looking like our father. And since Monique left, girls had been hanging around him.

They all went to the pharmacy with Carrot. Colin stared and stared. He was grinning.

There were no girls at the house on Cota Street when they got back. Just our father, who was sleeping. Colin kept telling Ratboy and Carrot that he had to get enough money together so he could get out of town. He had to be with Monique and their baby. It was killing him. She was there. Waiting. And all alone. He stood on the back porch at the house on Cota Street and smoked a menthol cigarette. He faced away from Carrot who was nervous and Ratboy, who was thinking about video games. He stared at the stars and said, "Seven years out of state and they can't do shit to me." He made plans out loud. A brief lucidity provided a faultless plan with intricate details. "Write this down!" he told Carrot, who fumbled with a pen and paper. Ratboy was good-natured and said he would help.

If Carrot and Ratboy hadn't been so stoned on O'Neel weed,

they would have known: *Colin had lost his edge.* His hands shook now. Ratboy had never been too smart himself. But it wasn't his fault. His head had been bashed in one too many times. His daddy was a mean drunk.

Some girls showed up for Colin. They had mushrooms in a bag. They shared with Ratboy and Carrot. Colin said he didn't want any. Some boys showed up. And then more girls. One of the girls was a cute brunette who was too young to be burned-out yet. She wanted Carrot to smoke meth with her. She was naïve and thought all rednecks had more money than white trash. Carrot would have done whatever the brunette wanted. His mother's tall can and her pain pills were long gone. He wasn't sure where his truck was. The girl had already talked him into buying meth from her. Carrot was getting confused. He had to work in the morning.

Colin's eyes were glazed over. Every night was the same on Cota Street. Two girls were making out loudly—the triangles of their thong underwear peeking out of their low-cut jeans. He shivered. Called to Ratboy. Told him to get one of the girls to drop them off a block from the pharmacy.

At 1 a.m. Colin used a bolt cutter on the lock at the back door. Ratboy waited in the bushes. The man in the house next door heard his dogs barking and Colin rattling the chain. He yelled out to him. Colin ran away—the pharmacist, who lived next door, fired his shotgun.

Colin crawled into a ditch where rainwater gathered. His wounds bled slowly. Ratboy couldn't find him. The man heard him clumsily searching and shot blindly into the bushes once again. Ratboy had to leave. The girl who had driven them was long gone. Adrenaline pumped through Colin's body. It was three hours before the police came.

A wheelbarrow full of dead weeds and grass clippings had been dumped into the ditch. The smell entered Colin's foggy hallucinations. He thought he was smoking cigarettes with Ratboy and cheering for Mima's goal. Walking next to me down the hill. He tried to call out. He thought about driving to Montana to get Monique—taking her up to the O'Neel property. They could live off the land for a while—raise their son together. He kept his head up for longer than most would have. His hands pulled at the loose dirt. He had meant to tell me something. He had meant to tell me Mima was coming with us. Walking next to us down the hill. But slowly, slowly he slipped back in the ditch—gulped swamp water and green algae. Mosquitoes buzzed around his head. The rain—it poured down.

Colin O'Neel died next to an aluminum drainpipe. He was twenty years old.

31

OILY SNAKES, SCARED HAMSTERS, AND NIGHTMARE SPIDERS

The ride back to David from St. Louis was long. I left the truck with a blown head gasket in Shelton, Nebraska. I got on a Greyhound. I slept and cried and slept and cried. I dreamed of oily snakes and spiders that lived inside my skull and stood up on high, spindly legs. The spiders spit out black-ink poison. They were terrified. *Mother, check my bed for spiders*, I used to ask her, *Please.* When I was little. So they wouldn't crawl inside my head while I was sleeping. So they wouldn't make a nest there and be afraid to come out. They would hurt me while trying to escape. I was sure of it. Animals scratched and bit when they were frightened and cornered. I'd seen Mima's hamster run up inside the couch. She grasped after him blindly with her fingers outstretched. He was backed into a corner. A dangerous place for a hamster. He bit her. He bit her hard. His sharp incisors connected underneath her skin. Because the animal was panicked.

I remembered catching a black garter snake with a red stripe down his back. I remembered playing with him until his good nature wore thin. He did not like to be put into a shoebox with no out-hole. I held on to him for too long. I looked down and he was biting me without teeth. I felt sorry. The bite did not hurt. I flung him away. I was left with a guilty feeling and a swipe of snake slobber on my arm. He slithered under a rhododendron bush and glared. My hands were left covered in stinky snake oil. He was a good snake, but I had pushed him too far.

Brady met me at the Greyhound station with lonely eyes. But he was getting stronger. I watched the gray skies and green trees from inside his truck. In Washington, everything was foreign and strange and wet-looking. The weather shocked me. It should have been hot. Hot enough to melt my breath away. But the air was dry and not weighed down with a sodden feeling. There were damp chills. And cool, fresh air. I remembered casual clothes and the way that David girls stripped down to the bare essentials at the first sign of spring. Midriffs smiled. Thighs were encased in short denim cutoffs. Pregnant teenagers sweated. The mud softened. It stuck on every truck. Fans of dirt spread out behind each tire. Nomads escaped to the hills. Daffodils bloomed in cow pastures.

I shivered and watched all the tourists move around the big, new store that would squash all the little, old ones. Brady disappeared inside the sprawling building to find Fitz. I waited in the truck where I couldn't get my blood going. The cold wind laughed. It blew the evergreens around like little sticks. The storm continued. I heard the screeching of the machinery. Nobody flinched but me.

My insides were ice, and my teeth chattered. The metal gears were tired. I could hear them grinding against one another. They needed oil. They sped up anyway. They reached the type of speed and madness that does not look back. That must consume voraciously. The sound of metal clanking on metal droned on and on in my ears. The engine labored. It leached the energy from my body. It could not go on like this. Something had to give. Purple circles dug out homes underneath my eyes.

I knew it wasn't smart for me to come back to David. But I couldn't leave Dad all alone.

I hoped everything had blown over. Brady dropped me off on Cota Street and told me he'd be back. The note Jimmy James had sent me was still in my chipped, blue dresser drawer. Piled on top of musty-smelling clothes. I'd left it there in my hurry to leave. The folded yellow paper a boy had given to me at a bus stop. I recognized Jimmy James's handwriting. The note was written in pencil. I heard his strong voice echo back at me while I read the words: *You've gotta lay low for a while. I'll be back.*

It wasn't a dream. I had really left David. St. Louis had not been a lonely vision. Jimmy James was not waiting for me. The machine was still up and running one thousand miles a minute. But this time I was one hundred years older. The things that should have made me scream backed up in my head. I couldn't let them come out of my mouth. They curled inward.

They coiled around my brain like oily snakes. They ran inside my skull like scared hamsters—nightmare spiders. They wouldn't go away.

BACK TO THE HILLS

Dad wanted to go up high where the fossils lay imbedded in silt. Brady, Fitz, and I went with him. My father was a man of few words. He gestured hesitantly through the screen of trees at a doe and her yearling. He didn't feel his legs as he climbed. He tried to walk out of his misery in the timber company land. We all wondered if a stranger from overseas would buy it. We knew we were living on borrowed time. We knew that soon lawn mowers and fertilizers and BMWs would crowd the forested floodplain. We searched for small, hidden meadows where deer ate grass. We found still ponds where temporarily landlocked sea-run cutthroat got fat. The sunshine settled into our bones—it loosened a few tears. They fell without our noticing. We forgot about the crammed church and the small, hasty funeral. The people who didn't know. We tried to eat our bread and meat and look down the sides of the canyon—hear the Skokomish River—watch for

La Llorona. My molars throbbed. I threw my food down angrily. I sat across from Brady at a boulder. Some part of our grief was shameful—because of how my brother lived. And then how he died. Because we were not only mourning the loss of my only brother. We were also, in a sense, grieving for the great damage of a life wasted.

I lay down on the rocks. I couldn't look at the men around me. I missed Annie and Monique and Mima and finally, earth shatteringly: *Mother.* A stick dug into my side. I didn't move. We were quiet as the sunshine warmed us. Calm and sad and muted—afraid that the sound of our voices would take the light away. We would ruin it somehow. I tried to think of Granny—how her leathery face had howled about the family name—the loss of the grandson whom she had carried such desperate hopes for.

A bleak emptiness lay where all the screaming had been—the engine with its fan belt off, the transmission knocking. All the anger subsided into shaky, frantic fear that paralyzed my body as I twisted on the rocks. I felt injured and angry. My mind swirled with David and my memories. The good and the bad—the complex warehouse of unrecorded facts. I was an immigrant who could never go back. I did not belong anywhere. I wanted a sacred place to hold my head high. The ancient Chinook salmon fossils watched. The king salmon had been caught in the midst of spawning. Their images stayed encased in the crumbling rock. They had been there a million years. Dad kept staring at the swallows diving in and out of their holes in an embankment. His Adam's apple bobbed up and down. He cleared his throat as if to speak. But nothing came out.

I thought about Brady getting fired. How they'd asked him a lot of questions and saw Fitz's shaved head when he came to tell him about Colin, and that I was back in town. His supervisors looked closely at his tattoos—the patches on his jacket. They remembered reading about Jimmy James in the newspaper. They told Brady not to come back.

I'd been packing his Bronco with my things.

Fitz had enlisted. He was going to be an army ranger—a ground troop. He would be dead soon. Or like the others who came back wary and broken. He knew there was no oil left. And they would use his blood to get more. The two would mix together in a black-and-red oxblood lake.

I thought about that color—how it meant good and bad things at the same time. Like the blood at birth. But how birth sometimes meant death. And how the man at the library so long ago described crude oil spilled out over water on a river delta in Nigeria. And the sunset over it while it burned. And the low beams turned the polluted water into a churning red with dark shadows.

Joey was going to join Brady as soon as the ferry docked in Bellingham. Nadine didn't answer her phone anymore.

"If everything works out, you can go to Montana with us," I coaxed Dad quietly. I was thinking of Monique and my new nephew, Colin James. Dad didn't answer. He handed me a letter and a handgun instead. The letter was folded three times. He told me to read it later.

I knew Dad would never leave the hills. For better or worse. He would take his insurance money and buy supplies. He would hunt his own food. Cook over an open fire. He would sniff at the boundaries—view the strange houses that popped up with astonishing speed. He would shake his head at all the people— their thin skin and cruel stupidity. He would sneak back to his cabin like a beaten dog and keep his mouth shut. He would grow strange and tireless in his bitter solitude. He would wait.

The machine was up and running smoothly. It was oiled with Annie's and Colin's blood.

All thoughts of a future had long ago been buried in cement.

I got up and stared at the fish. I thought of the things Dad told me so long ago. About resources and devastation. About powerful men and trouble. And how if you didn't fight, there could only be a land sucked dry and a world that was stormy and barren and drained. And then it would be too late—the fighting would be frightened desperation.

I remembered, *It is worse to fight a man who is scared than to fight a man who is bigger than you. A man who has nothing to lose will do crazy things. Anything. Adrenaline takes over—the fight mode. He might bite and scratch and use scissors to stab you. Kick you in the groin. Stick your own switchblade in your back while you're doubled over.*

We left the salmon to keep watch from the rocks. There would be many storms to come. The fish saw the confusion, and the cold. They sensed the coming heat. The wind, and droughts, and floods. The hunger and despair. The mass extinctions and lack of adaptations. The ice age that would come whether we liked it or not. My father planned his cabin. It was becoming more and more clear.

From the trail down, I listened for the sounds of war to come along with the wet scent of the far-off, foggy sea air. The fresh blood mingled with the strong, painful scent of Douglas fir. I smelled the misty spring rain and heard the sounds of the train and felt the rumbling rumors. I listened for that scream in a cheating wind. That shout on the playground that I never heard.

That night I sat alone in the house on Cota Street. I waited for the sunset. And the time when every moment became *one* moment and then got lost. I had come up against a wall. I had to turn and fight. Luckily, I was a fighter. Luckily, I was born for it.

I closed my eyes against the waning light. I saw the blood dry and harden behind my eyelids. Colin's stains were still on the cheap paint. I dreamed of legions of shaved heads and ships docking at discreet western ports. The men buried in the hills moaned and turned and grew restless. Soon, they would rise along with the rest. The stories circled my head. They agitated my every move. The images would not leave. It was in my blood. Words did not come easily. Words did nothing.

The body of the eighteen-year-old man from Angel Road was controlled in shackles and chains as the guards transported him from the county jail to the Washington State Correctional Facility in Matlock. They did not give him my letters. They photographed and documented his tattoos. They asked him questions about his affiliations. He knew they wasted precious time.

Jimmy James Blood's shoulders sagged from the knowledge of what they did not know—at what they would not understand until it was too late. His spirit boiled from inside his handcuffs and clenched teeth.

Monique sat entombed in a lonely silence across state lines. She tuned her acoustic alone in her room. She knew I was coming to tell her the news. She wore black eyeliner to school. She did not look at her classmates directly. She did not look at anyone directly.

Dad watched from the tavern by the train tracks as his house burned down in hot flames—as the fire licked hungrily at the dry wood.

On the side of the highway, Brady's Bronco sat with the engine running. Sam Cook sang "Summertime" as the windshield fogged up.

Dad watched the smoke make shadows on the cracked pavement of Cota Street. The flames burned the old blood, the broken glass, and the memories we left there: *a bloodstained baseball bat and a pair of fourteen-eye oxbloods.* It happened more quickly than I thought it would. I clambered up the ladder and into the crawl space. The window at the end had always been broken—the glass Colin had kicked through so long ago.

I jumped.

The ground flew at me. The stars shone brilliantly. I was screaming—my hair a golden flag of battle. The wind slapped my face—the cold air rolled up my body in waves. Just for a moment, I was the red-ocher glow and the sooty smoke. Before the fire overcame the wooden frame, I readied myself to run. Aerosol cans exploded as I hit the ground. I was frightened, but . . . I knew my boots would take the shock.

Acknowledgments

It's possible this book would never have been published without Jonathan Evison, who accepted an unsolicited manuscript after I was hours late to his workshop. For a reason I can only call kindness, he accepted the story and actually read it. He championed the book and gave it to Harry Kirchner, who believed in the novel before it was truly born, offered editorial advice, and found it a home.

Thank you to everyone at Counterpoint, Catapult, and Soft Skull who helped make the writing better: Mikayla Butchart and Jennifer Alton, who helped smooth out all the rough edges, and Jordan Koluch, who put up with my last-minute edits.

Also thank you to everyone who helped much earlier in the process:

Carmen Hoover, who offered advice and assistance along with the spring 2002 creative writing class at Olympic College Shelton;

Alejandra Abreu (I came to you with a backpack full of papers, and you said you would help); Rana Becker, who read numerous drafts and kept believing in the story; tutors at The Evergreen State College Writing Center, who helped edit the bits and pieces we could cover in under an hour; Tobi Vail, who encouraged me to keep moving forward and then showed me how; Sara Peté and numerous other librarians at various Timberland Regional Libraries, who helped set up readings; Meagan Macvie, who helped edit and posted an interview on her blog; and Bobby Brown, who offered technical advice on the ins and outs of murder.

Portions of this novel were completed during a fiction residency at the Vermont Studio Center. Thank you to everyone who supports fellowships, and also Jane Hamilton, the visiting writer, who read early chapters and offered careful criticism. I completed additional work during a creative writing retreat at The Evergreen State College taught by Rebecca Brown and a feminism class taught by Therese Saliba and Lin Nelson, and I received general encouragement from many, many additional professors and students at Evergreen. Thanks to everyone who kept coming to my readings and supported me over the years: you know who you are.

Additionally, I can't forget the ghosts in the rain who shared their stories, the ghosts downtown who wouldn't leave me, and some among the Douglas fir, who follow me still. I wish you the best of luck, and I hope you find what you are looking for.

Most importantly, thank you to my son, Walter, who was such a patient toddler throughout the editorial process. You are the best thing that ever happened to me.

MELISSA ANNE PETERSON grew up in a rainy working-class logging town in Washington State. She received a BA and BS in writing and biology from The Evergreen State College and an MS from the University of Montana. She has worked in endangered species recovery in Washington and Montana for twelve years. Her writing has been published by *Camas Magazine*, *Flyway: Journal of Writing & Environment*, *Oregon Quarterly*, and Seal Press. Find out more at melissaannepeterson.com.